Luc scanned t
with a distract
even to himsel
looking for.

Then he saw it.

Piano prodigy…pregnant? The photo was a blurry shot of Abby walking down a street in London. The newspaper had helpfully added a red circle to highlight the slight swell of her middle.

It took up only a few inches of space on the third page of the arts section. Abby, Luc realized, was hardly news anymore.

Yet she was, it seemed, pregnant. And he knew without even a flicker of doubt that if there was indeed a baby, then it was his.

He pushed the paper away, unfocused, unseeing, his mind spinning with thoughts he could barely articulate. The coffee at his elbow grew cold and the sun rose in the sky, casting longer and longer shadows on the floor.

Finally, as if shaking himself from a dream, Luc rose. He reached for his cell phone, flicked it open and punched buttons. When his assistant answered, he spoke tersely. "I need the jet. This morning."

Luc snapped his cell shut and gazed out at the River Seine winding through the city, the cherry trees just beginning to blossom. Then, turning away from the charming sight, he prepared to pack for his trip to England…to find Abby.

All about the author...
Kate Hewitt

KATE HEWITT discovered her first Harlequin romance on a trip to England when she was thirteen, and she's continued to read them ever since. She wrote her first story at the age of five, simply because her older brother had written one and she thought she could do it, too. That story was one sentence long—fortunately they've become a bit more detailed as she's grown older.

She studied drama in college, and shortly after graduation moved to New York City to pursue a career in theater. This was derailed by something far better—meeting the man of her dreams, who happened also to be her older brother's childhood friend. Ten days after their wedding they moved to England, where Kate worked a variety of different jobs—drama teacher, editorial assistant, youth worker, secretary and, finally, mother.

When her oldest daughter was one year old, Kate sold her first short story to a British magazine. Since then she has sold many stories and serials, but writing romance remains her first love—of course!

Besides writing, she enjoys reading, traveling and learning to knit—it's an ongoing process, and she's made a lot of scarves. After living in England for six years, she now resides in Connecticut with her husband, her three young children and the possibility of one day getting a dog.

Kate loves to hear from readers. You can contact her through her Web site, www.kate-hewitt.com.

Kate Hewitt

COUNT TOUSSAINT'S BABY

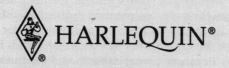

TORONTO • NEW YORK • LONDON
AMSTERDAM • PARIS • SYDNEY • HAMBURG
STOCKHOLM • ATHENS • TOKYO • MILAN • MADRID
PRAGUE • WARSAW • BUDAPEST • AUCKLAND

Recycling programs
for this product may
not exist in your area.

ISBN-13: 978-0-373-12937-9

COUNT TOUSSAINT'S BABY

First North American Publication 2010.

First published in the U.K. under the title
Count Toussaint's Pregnant Mistress.

Copyright © 2009 by Kate Hewitt.

COUNT TOUSSAINT'S BABY

To Anna and Brenda, for giving my girls a love of music. Thank you for all you do!

CHAPTER ONE

THE applause had ended and a hushed silence came over the concert hall, a wonderful expectancy that gave the room—and Abigail Summers—an almost electric excitement.

She took a breath, her fingers poised over the keys of the grand piano on the centre stage of the Salle Pleyel in Paris, closed her eyes, and then began to play.

The music flowed from her soul through her fingers, filling the room with the haunting, tormented sounds of Beethoven's twenty-third sonata. Abby was not conscious of the audience who sat in enthralled silence, who had paid nearly a hundred euros simply to listen to her. They melted away as the music took over her body, mind and soul, a passionate force both inside her and yet separate from her. Seven years of professional playing and a lifetime of lessons had taught her to completely and utterly focus on the music.

Yet, halfway through the *Appassionata*, she became… aware. There was no other word for the feeling that someone was watching her. Of course, several-hundreds of people were watching her, but this—*he*, for she knew instinctively it was a he—was different. Unique. She could feel his eyes on her, even though she didn't know how. Why.

Who.

Yet she didn't dare look up or lose her focus, even as her

cheeks warmed and her skin prickled, her body reacting with sensual pleasure to a kind of attention she'd never experienced and couldn't even be certain was real.

She found herself longing for the piece to end, all twenty-four minutes of it, so she could look up and see who was watching her. How could this be happening? she wondered with a detached part of her mind even as the music rippled from under her fingers. She'd never wanted a piece to end, had never felt the attention of one person like a spotlight on her soul.

Who was he?

Or was she just being fanciful, thinking that someone was there? Someone different. Someone, she felt strangely, for whom she'd been waiting her whole life.

Finally the last notes died away into the stillness of the hushed hall, and Abby looked up.

She saw and felt him immediately. Despite the glare of the stage lights and the sea of blurred faces, her eyes focused immediately on him, her gaze drawn to him as if by a magnet. There was something almost magnetic about it, about him. She felt as if her body were being irresistibly pulled towards him even though she remained seated on the piano bench.

He gazed back, and in the few seconds she'd had to look upon him her buzzing brain gathered only a few details: a mane of dark, slightly raggedly kept hair, a chiselled face, and most of all blue eyes, bright, intense, *burning*.

Abby was conscious of the rustling of concert programs, people shifting in their seats, the wave of speculative concern that rippled through the room. She should have started her next piece, a fugue by Bach, but instead she was sitting here motionless, transfixed, wondering.

She didn't have the luxury of asking questions or seeking answers. Taking a deep breath, she willed herself to focus once more, to think of nothing but the music. The beauty.

Yet even as she began the piece by Bach, the audience

seeming to sit back in their seats with a collective sigh of relief, she was still conscious of him, and she wondered if she would see him again.

Jean-Luc Toussaint sat in his seat, every muscle tense with anticipation, with awareness, with hope. It was an emotion he hadn't felt in a long time—months at the very least, most likely years. He hadn't felt anything at all. Yet when Abigail Summers, the world-renowned pianist prodigy, had come onto the stage he'd felt hope leap to life inside him, had felt the ashes of his old self stir to life in a way he had never thought to experience again.

He'd seen pictures of her, of course; there was a rather artistic photograph of her outside the Salle Pleyel, a graceful silhouette of her at the piano. Yet nothing had prepared him for the sight of her coming onto the stage: her head held high, her glossy, dark hair pulled into an elegant chignon, the un-relieved black evening-gown she wore swishing about her ankles. Nothing had prepared him for the response he'd felt in his own soul, for the emotions—hope, even joy—to course through him.

He'd tried to dismiss the feelings as mere desperate ima-ginings, for surely he was desperate? It was six months since Suzanne had died, and little more than six hours since he'd discovered her letters and realized the truth about her death. Had felt the blame and the guilt, corrosive and consuming.

He'd left the chateau and all of its memories for Paris, avoiding his flat or any of the remnants of his former life. He'd come to this concert as an act of impulse; he'd seen a billboard advert and he'd wanted to lose himself in something else, to not have to think at all, or even feel.

He couldn't feel; he was poured out, empty, barren of emotion…until Abigail Summers had crossed the stage.

And when she'd played… Admittedly, the *Appassionata*

was one of his favourite sonatas; he understood Beethoven's frustration, the inevitability of the composer's disability and his own inability to stop its relentless development. He felt that way about his own life, the way things had spiralled downwards, out of his control…and without him even realizing it until it was too late—far, far too late.

Yet Abigail Summers brought a new energy and emotion to the piece, so much so that Luc found his hands clenching into fists, his eyes burning as he gazed at her, as if he could compel her to look up and see him.

And then she did. Luc felt a sudden jolt of recognition, which seemed impossible, as he'd never met or even seen her before. Yet as their eyes met he felt as if something long-missing had finally slid into place, as if the world had righted itself, as if *he* had finally righted himself and been made whole.

He felt hope.

It was a heady, wonderful, addictive feeling. It was also frightening, feeling so much, and yet still he wanted more. He wanted to forget everything that had happened, all the mistakes he'd made in the last six years. He wanted that blissful oblivion, to lose himself in this look, this woman, even if only for a time. Even if it couldn't last.

Their eyes met and locked, the moment stretching and spiralling between them. Then, as the audience grew restless, she looked back down, and after a tense moment—he didn't think he imagined that hesitation—she began to play.

Luc sat back and let the music wash over him. That one look had caused a deep hunger to open up inside him, a restless longing to connect with another person, with her, as he never truly had with anyone. Yet even as the hunger took hold of him he felt the more familiar hopelessness wash over him. How could he want someone, have someone, when he had nothing, absolutely nothing, left to give?

* * *

Abby sank onto the stool in front of the mirror in her dressing-room backstage. She let out a shaky breath and closed her eyes. The concert had been endless. She'd paced restlessly all through intermission, which had hardly benefitted her playing in the second half. If her father and manager had been present, he would have urged her to drink some water, to relax and focus. *Think of the music, Abby.* Always the music. She'd never been allowed to think of anything else; before tonight she hadn't known she wanted to.

Yet seeing that man—*who was he?*—had caused something inside her to shift, loosen, and she was aware of a need she'd never felt before. A need to see him, talk to him, touch him, even.

She shivered, a reaction both of longing and a little fear. Her father wasn't here, he was back at the hotel with a head cold, and for once she didn't want to think of the music. She wanted to think of the man. Would he come? Would he try to get backstage and see her? There were always several dozen appreciative fans who tried to meet her; some sent flowers, congratulations, invitations. Abby accepted the gifts and refused the invitations. That was her father's strict policy; part of her allure, he insisted, was her sense of remoteness. For seven years she'd been kept at a distance from her public, from life itself, in order to build her reputation as the talented and elusive Abigail Summers, Piano Prodigy.

Abby made a face at her reflection in the mirror. She'd always hated that nickname, a name coined by the press that made her feel like a trained poodle, or perhaps something a bit more exotic, a bit more *remote*, as her father had always wanted.

Right now she had no desire to be remote. She wanted to be found, known. By him.

Ridiculous, her mind scoffed. It had been but a moment, a single look. She hadn't dared look at him again; she'd been too afraid, fearful of both seeing and not seeing him again. Both possibilities seemed dangerous. Even so, the memory of those few shared seconds resonated through her body, every nerve twanging with remembered feeling.

She'd never felt that way before. She'd never felt so… alive. And she wanted to feel it again. Wanted to see him again.

Would he come?

A light, perfunctory knock sounded at the door and one of the Salle Pleyel's staff poked her head through. 'Mademoiselle Summers, *recevez-vous des visiteurs*?'

'I…' Abby's mouth was dry, her mind spinning. Was she receiving visitors? The answer, of course, was no. It was always no. *Send them a signed program, Abby, and be done with it. You can't be just another girl. You need to be different.*

'Are there many?' she finally asked, in flawless French, and the woman gave a little shrug.

'A few…a dozen or so. They want your autograph, of course.'

Abby felt a sharp little stab of disappointment. Somehow she knew this man would not want her autograph. He wasn't a fan. He was…what? *Nothing*, her mind insisted almost frantically, even as her heart longed for it to be otherwise. 'I see.' She swallowed, looked away. 'All right. You may send them in.'

The concert-hall manager, Monsieur Dupres, appeared in the doorway, a look of disapproval on his dour face. 'It was my understanding that Mademoiselle Summers did not accept visitors.'

A crony of her father, Abby thought with a cynical smile. He had them in every concert hall.

'I believe I know whether I accept visitors or not,' she replied coolly, although her palms were damp and her heart was thudding. She didn't question staff and she didn't make a fuss. That was her father's job. Her job was simply to play. And that had been enough, until now. At least she'd always thought it had. Right now she was hungry, anxious, craving more than the safe, ordered, *managed* existence she'd been living for as long as she could remember. She met the man's gaze directly. 'Send them in.'

'I don't think—'

'Send them in.'

His lips tightened and he gave a shrug before turning away. 'Very well.'

Abby smoothed her hair back with her palms and checked her gown. In the mirror the black silk made her skin look pale, almost ghostly, her grey eyes huge and luminous.

Another knock sounded at the door and she turned, smiling even as her heart sank.

It wasn't him.

None of them was, it was a cluster of middle-aged women and their sheepish husbands smiling and chattering as they thrust out their programs for her to sign.

What had she expected? Abby asked herself as she chatted back and gave the requisite signatures. That he would find her backstage, and come bearing a glass slipper? Did she think she lived in a fairy tale? Had she really expected him to find her at all?

Suddenly the whole notion seemed ridiculous, the moment when their eyes had met imagined and laughable. She'd probably made up the whole thing. The stage lights were usually so bright she couldn't make out any faces in the audience. Was he even real?

Abby felt her face warm with private humiliation. The crowd of well-wishers trickled away, followed by a glowering Monsieur Dupres, and Abby was left alone.

Lonely.

The word popped into her mind, and she forced it away. She was not lonely. She had a busy, full life as one of the world's most sought-after concert pianists. She spoke three languages fluently, had visited nearly every major city in the world, had legions of adoring fans—how could she possibly be lonely?

'Yet I am,' she said aloud, and winced at the sound of her forlorn voice in the empty dressing-room. She only had herself to talk to.

Slowly, reluctantly, she reached for her coat, a worn duffel that looked incongruous over her evening gown. She could hear the sound of the night-janitor starting to sweep the hallway outside, the concert-hall staff trickling away into the evening and their own lives.

What would she do? Take a taxi back to the hotel, perhaps have a glass of hot milk while she went over the evening's events with her father, and then to bed like the good little girl she was. Her fingers fumbled on the buttons of her coat.

She didn't want to play out the staid script her life had become, didn't want the role her father had given her years ago. Seeing that man, whoever he was, had awakened in her a need to experience more, be and know more. To actually live life.

Even if just for a night.

She sighed, trying to dismiss the feelings, for what could she do? She was twenty-four years old, alone in Paris, the evening ahead of her, and she had no idea what to do, how to slake this thirst for life, for experience.

Monsieur Dupres knocked on her dressing-room door once more. 'Shall I have the night porter summon a taxi?'

Abby opened her mouth to accept, then found herself shaking her head. 'No, thank you, Monsieur Dupres. It's a lovely evening out. I'll walk.'

The manager's heavy brows drew together in an ominous frown. 'Mademoiselle, it is raining.'

Abby refused to back down. This was a tiny, insignificant act of defiance, yet it was hers. 'Still.' She smiled. 'I'll walk.'

With a shrug Monsieur Dupres turned away. With her fingers clenched around her handbag, Abby left the dressing room and the concert hall behind her, stepping out into the cool, damp night alone.

Alone; she was completely alone on the deserted Rue du Faubourg St Honoré. The pavement was slick with rain, the lights of the speeding taxis washing the road in pale yellow.

Abby looked around, wondering what to do. Her hotel, a modest little establishment, was half a mile away. She could walk, she supposed, as she'd told Monsieur Dupres she would do. A little stab of disappointment needled her. She wanted to experience life, so she was walking home alone in the rain—how ridiculous.

Her heels clicked on the pavement as she started down the street. A man in a trenchcoat hurried by, his collar turned up, and Abby glimpsed a pair of lovers entwined in the shelter of a doorway; the woman's upturned face was misted and glowing with rain.

Abby walked, conscious more than ever of how alone she was. A woman dripping with furs and jewels stepped out of the bright lobby of an elegant hotel, her haughty, made-up face glowering with disdain at the world around her.

Abby slowed to a stop, the light from the lobby pooling, golden, around her feet. Through the ornate glass doors she could see a marble foyer and a huge crystal chandelier. As the door swooshed shut she caught the sound of clinking crystal, the trill of feminine laughter.

Without thinking about what she was doing—or why— Abby caught the closing door and thrust it open once more, even as the night porter leapt to attention a second too late.

She dismissed him with a wave of her hand and slipped inside, the warmth and light of the hotel enveloping her with a strange new, electric excitement as she stood uncertainly in the doorway.

She'd been to hotels before all over the world. She was utterly familiar in foyers such as these, could issue commands to a bellboy or concierge in many different languages. Yet now as she stood there alone, uncertain, everything felt new. Different. For this time she was alone, no one knew who or where she was, and she could do as she pleased.

The question was, do what?

'Mademoiselle…?' A bellboy started forward, eyebrows raised in query. Abby lifted her chin.

'I'm looking for the bar.'

The man nodded and gestured to a room off to the right panelled in dark wood. Abby nodded her thanks and started towards the long, mahogany bar, still with no idea what she was doing…or why.

She slid onto a leather stool, her hands clasped in front of her. The bartender, dressed in a tuxedo, was slowly polishing a tumbler. He glanced at her, taking in her worn coat and the diamanté straps of her evening gown visible from the open collar. Expressionless, he raised an eyebrow.

'Would you like a drink?'

'Yes.' Abby swallowed. She'd ordered wine, she'd drunk champagne; on occasion she'd had a nameless cocktail at one function or another. Now she wanted something different.

'I'll have…' She swallowed, her mouth dry. 'A martini.'

'Straight or on the rocks?'

Oh, great. Did she want it with ice? What was even *in* a martini? And why had she ordered one? She had a feeling she wasn't going to like it. 'Straight,' she said firmly. 'With an…olive.' She had a vague collection that it came with olives. If she didn't like the drink, at least she'd have something to eat.

The bartender turned away, and Abby's gaze roved over the bar. Only one other person was sitting there, all the way at the other end, and before he even looked up or acknowledged her presence—with a shock that felt like an icy finger trailing down her spine and diving into her belly—she knew.

Him.

CHAPTER TWO

SHE knew it was him; she felt it in that tremor of electric awareness that rippled through her body; every nerve and muscle was on high alert as her heart began to beat with slow, heavy, deliberate thuds. He sat on the last stool, a tumbler of whisky in front of him, his head bent.

Then he raised his head and Abby's breath caught in her throat, the sheer emotion of the moment turning her breathless and dizzy as he turned so that his gaze met and held hers, just as it had once before. For a long, taut moment neither of them spoke, they simply looked. The look went on far longer than it should have, than was appropriate for two strangers staring at each other in a bar. Still Abby could not look away. She felt as if she were suspended in time, in air, motionless and yet waiting.

'You're even lovelier in person.' He spoke in English with a faint French accent, his low voice carrying across the empty room. Shock rippled through her at the realization that he knew who she was; he recognized her. Of course, plenty of people recognized her. She was the Piano Prodigy, after all. Yet under the quiet heat of his gaze Abby knew he wasn't looking at her as a prodigy, or even a pianist. He was looking at her as a woman, and that felt wonderful.

'You remember me,' she whispered. Her voice trembled

and she blushed at the realization, as well as the revealing nature of the statement. She couldn't dissemble. She didn't know how to, and she wasn't even sure she wanted to.

He arched one eyebrow, with the flicker of a smile around his mouth and in his eyes. 'Of course I remember you,' he said, a gentle, teasing lilt to his voice—although Abby saw an intensity in his fierce blue eyes, the same intensity she'd seen in the concert hall and had responded to. 'And now I know you remember me.'

Her blush deepened and she looked away. The bartender had delivered her martini, complete with an olive pierced by a swizzle-stick, and she seized the drink as a distraction, taking far too large a sip.

She choked, gasping as the pure alcohol burned its way to her belly, and she returned the glass to the bar with an unsteady clatter.

She felt rather than saw the man move from his stool to the one next to hers, felt the heat emanating from his lean form, inhaled the woodsy musk of his cologne. And choked a bit more.

'Are you all right?' he murmured, all solicitude, although Abby thought she heard a hint of laughter lacing the words. She wiped her eyes and took a deep, cleansing breath.

'Yes. It…went down the wrong way.'

'That happens,' he murmured, and Abby knew he wasn't fooled. She decided she might as well be candid.

'Actually, I've never had a martini before,' she said, turning to look at him. 'I had no idea it would taste so…strong.' Now that he was here, just a few feet away from her, she took the opportunity to let her gaze sweep over him. He was tall, well over six feet, dwarfing her own five-eight frame. His hair was dark with a few streaks of grey near the temples, and long enough to raggedly reach his collar. His face held an austere beauty; the chiselled cheekbones, fiercely blue eyes and strong jaw all worked together to create an impression of strength, yet also, strangely, of suffering. He looked and walked like a man apart, a man marked by life's experience. By tragedy, perhaps.

Abby knew she should dismiss such impressions as fanciful, yet she could not. They were too strong, too real, just as the connection she'd felt between them at the concert and now in the bar felt real.

'Why did you order a martini?' he asked.

'I wanted to order what I thought was a sophisticated drink,' she admitted baldly. 'Isn't that ridiculous?'

He tilted his head, his smile deepening to reveal a devastating dimple in one cheek. His gaze swept over her worn coat, the black silk of her gown gathered around her ankles, one high-heeled sandal dangling from her foot. 'It surely is,' he agreed, 'considering how sophisticated you already are.'

Abby choked again, this time in laughter. 'You are quite the flatterer, Monsieur…?'

'Luc.'

'Monsieur Luc?'

'Just Luc.' There was a flat finality to his words that made Abby realize just how anonymous this conversation really was. She had no idea who he was beyond his first name. 'And I know who you are,' he continued. 'Abigail.'

'Abby.'

He smiled, a gesture that was strangely intimate, making warmth spread through Abby's body. A warmth she'd never experienced before but knew she liked trickled through her limbs like warm honey, making her feel languorous, almost sleepy, even though her heart still beat fast. It was a warmth that drew her to him even though she didn't move, made her believe in the fairy tale. This really was happening. This was real. She'd found him, here in this bar, and he'd found her. 'Abby,' he murmured. 'Of course.'

Of course. As if they knew each other, had known each other long before this moment, as if they'd been waiting for this moment. Abby felt she had been.

'So.' Again he smiled, no more than a flicker as he gestured towards the martini. 'What do you think?'

Abby made a face. 'I think I prefer champagne.'

'Then champagne you shall have.' With a simple flick of his wrist, Luc had the bartender hurrying over. A quick command in rapid French soon had him producing a dusty bottle of what Abby knew must be an outrageously expensive champagne and two fragile flutes. 'Will you share a glass with me?' Luc asked, and Abby barely resisted the impulse to laugh wildly.

In all her years playing in concert halls she'd never had an encounter like this. She'd never had any encounters at all, save the few carefully orchestrated conversations or program-signings her father arranged. They'd always made Abby feel like she was an exotic creature in a zoo to be watched, petted, admired and then left.

Caged, she realized. *I've felt caged all my life.* Until now. This moment felt free.

'Yes,' she said, surprised at how simple the decision was. 'I will.'

Luc led her to a cozy table for two in the corner of the deserted bar, and Abby sank onto the plush seat, watching as the waiter popped the cork and poured two glasses of champagne, the bubbles zinging wildly.

'To unexpected surprises,' Luc said, raising his glass.

Abby couldn't resist asking, 'Aren't all surprises unexpected?'

His smile curved his mobile mouth and glimmered in his eyes. 'So they are,' he agreed, and drank.

Abby drank too, letting the champagne slip down her throat and through her body. The bubbles seemed to race through every vein and artery. She stared at the bubbles in her glass and watched them pop against the side of the flute as she desperately thought of something to say.

She'd played in the concert halls of nearly every European capital, she could navigate airports, taxis and foreign hotels, yet in the presence of this man she felt tongue-tied, and even gauche, uncertain, unable to fully believe that this was even happening.

Yet it was.

She slid a sideways glance at him and saw that there was a particularly hard set to his jaw, a determined resoluteness that seemed at odds with his light tone, the glimmer of his smile. He possessed a hardness, Abby thought suddenly, a darkness that she didn't understand and wasn't sure she wanted to.

He downed the rest of his champagne, turning to smile at her, the darkness retreating to his eyes alone. 'I didn't expect to see you again. It is providence, is it not, that you came here?'

Providence. An act of fate, of God. Abby gave a little helpless shrug of assent. 'I don't know why I did. I usually take a taxi straight home after a concert.'

'But tonight you did not.'

'No.' The admission was no more than a breath of sound, and Luc's direct blue gaze met hers.

'Why not?'

'Because…' How could she explain that the single moment of seeing him in the concert hall had changed her, made her want and feel things she'd never felt before? That single glance had opened a well of yearning inside her, and she didn't know how it could be satisfied. 'Because I felt restless,' she finally said, and Luc nodded. Abby felt as if he understood everything she hadn't said.

'When I saw you,' he said in a low voice, rotating the stem of his champagne flute between his long, lean fingers, 'I felt something I have not felt in a long time.'

Abby's breath hitched and her fingers tightened around her own glass. 'What?' she asked. 'What did you feel?'

Luc opened up, surprising Abby with the bleak, stark honesty of his gaze. 'Hope.' He reached out to brush a still-damp tendril of hair from her cheek, his fingers barely touching her, yet still causing a wave of sensation to crash over her, dousing her to her core. 'Didn't you feel it, Abby? When you were at the piano and you saw me? I have never—' He stopped, then started again. 'It was like a current. Electric. Magical.'

'Yes,' she whispered, the word catching in her throat. 'I felt it too.'

'I am glad.' Luc's mouth quirked upwards in a tiny smile, although there was a curious bleakness to his words. 'It would be a sad thing if only one of us had felt it.' He reached for the champagne bottle and topped up both of their glasses, although Abby had hardly had a sip. 'Were you pleased with your performance tonight?'

'I don't know.' She took a tiny sip of champagne. 'I can't remember much of it.'

Luc laughed softly. 'Neither can I, to tell you the truth. When you came on stage and I saw you, the rest fell away. I was simply waiting for the moment when I could speak to you. I never thought it would be granted to me.'

'Why didn't you—?' Abby stopped, biting her lip to keep the words, the revealing question, from coming. Luc arched an eyebrow.

'Why didn't I…?' he prompted, and Abby shook her head. It didn't matter; he filled in the rest. 'Why didn't I come to see you after the performance?'

'Yes,' she whispered, the word no more than a whisper.

Luc stared into his glass for a moment, before lifting his head and giving her that direct gaze that seemed to reach right inside her and seize her soul. 'I didn't think I should.'

'But…' Abby couldn't think of what to say or ask, how to articulate that she'd wanted him to see her, had almost been expecting it. It sounded desperate, ridiculous. All they'd shared was one look—and now a glass of champagne. She set her half-empty glass down on the table. 'This doesn't seem—'

'Real? No. Perhaps not.' Luc glanced away for a moment, his mouth tightening, his jaw tensing. Abby felt as if she'd said the wrong thing and wished she could take it back. Then he turned back to her, smiling faintly, although she still sensed a certain sorrow in him, saw it in his eyes. 'Perhaps now is the time to be prosaic. Tell me about yourself.'

Abby shrugged, discomfited. 'If you read my bio in the program—'

'That might give me facts, but surely not the true essence of who you are?'

'I'm not sure I know what the true essence of myself is.' She made a face, eliciting a chuckle from him. 'That sounds rather mysterious.'

'And I meant to be prosaic. Tell me some other things, then,' he said as he gestured to the bartender, who hurried over. He glanced back at Abby. 'Have you eaten? Champagne on an empty stomach is not wise.'

As if on cue, Abby's stomach growled. She gave a little laugh. 'I haven't,' she confessed, and, flicking open the menu the bartender had provided, Luc quickly ordered. 'Is that all right?' he asked as he handed the menu back. 'I do not wish us to be bothered by such details as what food to order.' Abby gave a little shrug of assent, although she thought she'd heard him order *escargots* and she really wasn't fond of them. Somehow it didn't matter.

'So.' Luc propped his elbows on the table, his eyes seeming to glint and sparkle in the dim light. 'Tell me something. Tell me what your favorite colour is, or if you're scared of spiders or snakes. Did you have a dog growing up? Or a cat?' He took a sip of champagne, smiling at her over the rim of the glass. 'Or perhaps a fish?'

'None.' Abby reached for her own glass. 'And both.'

'Pardon?'

'No pets, and I'm scared of both spiders and snakes. At least, I don't like them very much. I haven't had much first-hand experience.'

'I suppose that's a good thing, then.'

'I never really thought about it.' Abby took a sip of cham-pagne. 'And what about you?'

'Am I scared of snakes or spiders?'

'No, I'll pick different questions.' She paused, thinking. What did she want to know about him? *Everything*; the answer sprang unbidden into her mind. She wanted to know him, to have the chance to know him. To go to sleep and wake up at his side… 'Do you snore?' she blurted, then blushed.

'Do I snore?' Luc repeated in mock outrage, one eyebrow arched. 'What a question. How should I know such a thing?' His lips curved into a smile that did curious things to Abby's insides, so that her stomach felt as quivery as a bowl of jelly. 'No one has ever told me I snore, at any rate.'

'Ah. Um…good.' She fiddled with her napkin, blushing, and wishing she wasn't. She stilled in shock when she felt Luc's hand cover her own, heavy and warm.

'Abby. You are nervous.'

'Yes,' she admitted. She forced herself to look at him. 'I'm not—I don't—' She swallowed. 'I don't usually accept invi-tations from strange men.'

'That is probably just as well,' Luc replied. 'But I promise you, you are safe with me.' He spoke with a raw, heartfelt sincerity that Abby could only believe. There was no ques-tion of doubt.

'I know.'

A black-jacketed waiter swept in silently with a tray. He didn't speak or even look at them, simply served the food while maintaining the aura of complete privacy they had been enjoying in the empty bar. When he left, Luc gestured down to their plates, to the delicate fan of asparagus amidst paper-thin slices of beef. 'Is this all right?'

'It looks delicious.' Abby picked up her fork and toyed with a piece of asparagus. 'Were you surprised to see me here?' she asked after a moment. 'In the bar?'

'You were like an apparition,' Luc told her. 'And yet, at the same time…' He paused, contemplating. 'It was as if I knew you would come, and I hadn't realized it until I saw you.'

'That's how I felt too,' Abby whispered, and Luc smiled.

'Perhaps,' he said slowly, almost regretfully, 'some things are meant to be.'

'Yes,' Abby agreed, and then added with an uncertain laugh, 'Except, as I said before, it hardly seems real.'

'Nothing good ever does,' Luc replied, and Abby glanced up, startled. It was a cynical statement, a belief born of suffering, and she wondered what had happened in Luc's life to make him say and believe such a thing. 'But tonight is as real as anything is.'

Abby nodded, wanting to lighten the mood. 'So I know you don't snore,' she said, popping a piece of asparagus into her mouth, 'but I don't know much else.' She paused, thinking. 'You're French.'

'Yes.'

'But you speak English almost perfectly.'

'As you do French.'

She accepted the compliment with a graceful nod. 'You've never heard me play before.'

'No.' He took a sip of wine. 'You're quite the detective.'

'You don't live in Paris?'

'No.'

Feeling relaxed and yet also a little bold, she added, 'You're rich.'

Luc gave a shrug of assent as only the rich could do. 'I have enough. As do you, I suppose?'

Abby nodded slowly. Yes, she had plenty of money. Her father took control of it, had done since she'd started playing professionally at seventeen. She had no idea how much money she had, or what kind of accounts it was kept in. Her father gave her spending money, and that had been enough. She'd never needed much; she liked to visit museums, buy cappuccinos in their cafés, or books. Her clothes were mostly picked by a stylist, who also took care of her hair, her nails, her make-up. She ate in restaurants and hotels, and sometimes on trains. There was little she needed, and yet somehow right now it all made her sad.

'You look rather wistful,' Luc murmured. 'I didn't mean to make you sad.'

'You didn't,' Abby said quickly. 'I was just…thinking.' She smiled, wanting to shift the attention from herself and her own dawning realizations about her life. She'd been happy, or at least content, until tonight…hadn't she? Yet in Luc's presence she was happier and more alive than she'd ever felt before. It made her aware of the deficiencies in her life, how before this her life had been mere existence, simply a waiting period for this moment. For him. 'You're not from Paris, so where are you from?'

Luc paused, and Abby had the sense that he didn't want to tell her. 'Down south,' he said finally. 'The Languedoc.'

'I've never been there.'

He gave a little smile. 'It has no concert halls.'

Her life had been defined by concert halls: Paris, London, Berlin, Prague, Milan, Madrid. She'd seen so many cities, so many gorgeous concert halls and anonymous hotel-rooms, and she felt it keenly now. The Languedoc. She wondered if he had a villa, or perhaps even a chateau. For some reason she imagined a quaint farmhouse with old stone walls, a tiled roof and brightly painted shutters amidst gently waving fields of lavender. A home. She gave a little laugh, shaking her head. Now she really was imagining things.

'Do you like it there?'

Luc paused. 'I did.' He spoke flatly, and Abby felt a new tension coil through the room. Then he shook it off with an easy shrug of his shoulders and smiled, leaning forward so Abby could see the lamplight glinting in his eyes; she inhaled the tang of his cologne. 'But enough of me. I want to know of you.'

Abby smiled back, feeling self-conscious. It seemed as if neither of them wanted to talk about themselves. 'Fire away.'

'I read in your biography that the *Appassionata* is one of your favourite pieces to play. Why?'

The question surprised her. 'Because it's beautiful and sad at the same time,' she finally said.

'And that appeals to you?'

'It's…how I've felt sometimes.' It was a strange admission, and one she hadn't meant to confess. One, she realized, she hadn't even acknowledged to herself. She loved music, loved playing piano, and yet somehow her life, the pinnacle of success, hadn't happened the way she had wanted it to. Or at least it hadn't felt the way she'd wanted it to. She felt like she was missing something, some integral part of life, of herself, that everyone else had.

Did she expect to find it here, with this man? Was such a thing possible? Abby took another sip of champagne. 'Why do you ask?'

'It is one of my favourite pieces, for the reason you just named, I suppose.' He nodded, smiling faintly. 'Beautiful and sad.'

Abby gave a little laugh. 'We both sound so gloomy! I love playing it, at any rate.'

The waiter returned to clear their plates, and then disappeared again as quietly as a cat. Abby was conscious of time passing; it must be nearing midnight. Her father, if he was awake, would be expecting her. Would he wait up? He had a cold, and had probably taken a sleeping tablet. He wouldn't worry, because for seven years her routine had been unfaltering—play the piano and return to the hotel, at first by chauffeured car and later by taxi.

When would she return tonight, and how? How would this evening end? The thought made her insides fizz with both wonder and worry, for she didn't want it to end. Not yet, not ever. This was a snatched moment, one night carved from a lifetime of music and duty—strange how those went together—and she wanted to savour it. She wanted it to last for ever.

'What are you thinking?' Luc asked, and before Abby could answer he continued, 'Are you thinking that time is running out? That we only have a few hours left?'

'How did you—?'

'Because I am thinking the same.' He smiled sadly. 'Perhaps that is all we are meant to have.'

'No!' The word was ripped from her, a confession, followed by another, deeper one: 'I don't want the evening to end.'

Luc gazed at her, his head tilted to one side, his eyes dark. 'Neither do I,' he replied quietly, and then, his tone turning wry, added, 'And so it won't. We have four more courses left, surely? This is France, after all.'

'*Bien sûr*,' Abby agreed after a moment, although she hadn't been talking about food and, she believed, neither had he. Yet what *had* she been talking about? What did she want? Her insides tightened, coiling in anticipation and awareness.

Luc smiled easily, and as if on cue the waiter brought the next course, a terrine of vegetables and herbs that was as light and frothy as air.

The evening passed in a pleasant blur of wine, food and easy conversation. It was easy, surprisingly easy, to talk to him, to slip off her heels and curl her feet under the folds of her gown, to try the *escargots* with a wrinkled nose as she confessed, 'But they're snails. I've never got over that somehow.'

'If you could do anything,' Luc asked as the waiter silently cleared their third course, 'what would it be?'

By this time Abby was all too relaxed, her chin propped in one hand, her eyes sparkling. 'Fly a kite,' she said, earning a surprised chuckle from Luc. 'Or learn to cook.'

'Fly a kite?' he repeated. 'Really?'

Abby shrugged, suddenly conscious of how childish such a wish seemed. 'When I was a child, I always saw them flying kites on Hampstead Heath.'

'Them?' Luc repeated softly, and Abby shrugged again.

'Them. Other children.'

'And you never flew a kite?'

'I was always on my way to piano lessons. Too busy.' The waiter returned with their dessert and Abby was glad of the reprieve. She hadn't meant to reveal quite so much with that question and its betraying answer. 'And cook, because food is so delicious and I've never learned how to make anything properly. What about you?' She took a spoonful of indulgently rich, dark-chocolate mousse. 'If you could do anything, what would it be?'

'Turn back time,' Luc stated matter-of-factly, and Abby started at how grim he sounded. Then he smiled and dipped his own spoon into the rich, chocolatey dessert. 'So I could have this evening with you all over again.'

Abby smiled, although she didn't think that was what he'd meant when he'd spoken about turning back time.

All too soon, however, the waiter returned on his silent cat's feet to clear away their chocolate mousse and pour the coffee in tiny porcelain cups, leaving a plate of *petits fours*, delicate and frosted pink, on the table.

The evening was almost over, Abby thought sadly. In a few minutes, a quarter of an hour perhaps, she would leave. She would find a taxi speeding down the near-empty Rue du Faubourg St Honoré, slip into its dark interior and give the driver the address of her own staid and respectable hotel half a mile away. Then she would pay the driver and walk through the deserted foyer of the hotel, avoiding the speculative looks of the bored bellboy and the silent censure of the concierge, praying that he would not tell her father, *'Mademoiselle est revenue trop tard...'*

Then she would forget this evening ever existed, and Luc—just Luc—would be nothing more than a distant memory, a dream.

Except... Except, she thought with a jolt, the evening didn't need to end at the bar. They could go somewhere else. Somewhere private.

A bedroom.

This was a hotel, after all. Was Luc staying here? Did he have a room? The questions, as well as their potential answers, left her dizzy. Was she, a woman who had barely been kissed, actually contemplating a night with this man? A one-night stand?

Yet it wouldn't be anything so sordid, because they knew each other. They were practically soulmates. The trite word made Abby grimace. Luc touched her hand, his caress light yet so very sure.

'Abby,' he said, 'what are you thinking?'

'That I don't want to go home,' Abby blurted. She felt herself flush and suddenly didn't care. 'I want to stay here with you.'

Luc frowned, a shadow of regret in his eyes. 'It is late. You should go.'

She reached out and curled her fingers around his wrist;

her thumb instinctively found his pulse. 'No.' Was she actually begging?

'It is better,' Luc said quietly. 'I…' He sighed, gazing down at her fingers still clasped on his wrist, and lightly, so lightly, traced the delicate skin of her inner wrist with his thumb. Abby nearly shuddered at the simple yet overwhelming contact.

'Is there any reason why we can't…be together?' she asked in a low voice, unable to look at him directly. She kept her gaze fastened on their clasped hands instead. 'You aren't… married?'

She felt Luc's fingers tighten, tense. 'No,' he said quietly. 'I'm not married.'

She strove for a lighter tone. 'Are you seeing someone?'

'No,' he said again, just as simply. 'There's no one.'

'Well.' Abby took a breath, gathered all her courage and looked up to meet Luc's dark gaze, offering him a smile. Offering herself. 'There's me.'

CHAPTER THREE

SHE was nervous, Luc saw, and he felt regret lash at him, a whip with a sting he'd felt far too many times already. He shouldn't have let it get this far, yet he'd been so amazed, so overjoyed, by her presence in the bar. It had felt, as he'd told her, like providence. A gift. And now she was offering herself, the greatest gift of all.

He could imagine it so easily. He wanted it so much. He pictured lacing his fingers through hers, drawing her up from her seat and away from the bar with its stale traces of cigarette smoke and spilled whisky and taking her to a room upstairs. The royal suite; he'd give her nothing less. He pictured her gliding through the room, slim and dark and elegant, and then he envisioned himself slipping those skinny little straps from her creamy shoulders and pressing a kiss against the pulse that now fluttered wildly at her throat. His fingers curled even now as he pictured it, aching, as every part of him was aching, with desire.

With need, the need to lose himself in a woman—this woman—for a moment, a night. For surely it could be no more? He had nothing more to offer; his heart felt as lifeless as a stone…except when it fluttered to life as he gazed at Abby. Yet he knew how little that was, and that was why the evening must end here, now. For Abby's sake.

'Abby.' He tried to smile, yet the movement hurt. He didn't want to let her go. She was the first good thing that had happened to him in so long, perhaps ever, and he couldn't bear to make her walk away. Not yet. *Please*, he offered in silent supplication, *not yet*.

Abby smiled and braced herself for rejection. Did he actually feel sorry for her? Had she just offered herself on a plate only to be pushed away?

'Do you know what you are saying?'

'Of course I do.' Brave words. She let her fingers skim his wrist. 'I wouldn't have said it otherwise.'

Luc gazed down at their entwined hands. Abby felt a wave of something dark and unrelenting emanate from him, a deep sorrow, an endless regret. 'You are a beautiful woman,' he said in a low voice, and disappointment stabbed at her with icy needles.

'But…?' she prompted sadly, and Luc looked up and smiled.

'I don't want to hurt you.'

'You won't.' More brave words, Abby knew. Foolish words, perhaps. Yet at that moment she felt like anything would be better, or at least more bearable, than walking away from Luc and the blossoming feeling of possibility he evoked in her just then.

Luc sighed, a heavy sound, and he shook his head slowly. Abby waited, holding her breath, hoping.

Then he stood, almost lazily reaching out to draw her to her feet, their fingers still twined.

'Where are you going?' Abby asked as she rose.

'The question,' he answered, tugging on her hand, 'is where are *we* going?'

Abby let him lead her out of the bar; the only sound was the swoosh of her gown around her ankles. Back in the lobby Luc had a rapid discussion with the concierge, and seconds later he led her to a bank of lifts. Abby's breath caught in her throat. She could hardly believe this was happening, that she was allowing it to happen, that she had asked for it to happen. She barely knew Luc, and yet…

Yet she knew him, perhaps better than she'd ever known anyone before. She couldn't turn away from this—him— even if she wanted to, even if she tried. She had no choice; her desire and need were too great.

The heady, surreal feeling didn't leave her as they stepped into the lift and Luc pressed the button for the top floor: the penthouse suite.

They rode in silence and Abby felt sure Luc could feel her heart beating; it felt as if it were thudding right out of her chest. She gave a sideways glance and saw how calm and un-concerned he looked. Determined, resolute even.

The lift came to a halt and the doors opened directly into the suite, which took up the whole floor.

'Come,' Luc said, and Abby followed him into the sump-tuous living-room, all velvet sofas and spindly gilt-tables, with about an acre of Turkish carpet. Abby stood in the doorway, mindlessly smoothing the silk of her gown, feeling shy and uncertain despite her earlier bravado.

She knew it wasn't the luxurious suite of rooms that put her on edge. In her years as a concert pianist she'd seen and experienced her fair share of luxury. No, it wasn't the room. It was the man.

He'd casually dropped the key-card the concierge had given him on a side table and shed his suit jacket, the muscles of his back and shoulders rippling under the smooth, silken fabric of his shirt. For a brief moment his body was in profile, his face in shadow. Abby didn't think she was imagining the grim set to his jaw, or the accompanying shiver that rippled through her body at the sight of him and the darkness ema-nating from within that beautiful body.

Yet then he turned to her with a little smile, his expression light and easy, and she wondered if she'd been imagining it after all.

'Aren't you going to come in?' he asked, laughter lurking in his voice, and Abby lowered her gaze.

'I…' She licked her lips. Now was not the time for cold feet, surely? 'I'm not sure.'

Luc frowned and strode towards her, his hands coming to curl around her shoulders. 'Abby…are you afraid?'

'Not…exactly.' Abby tried to laugh, but it came out wobbly and uncertain. 'Not of you,' she amended. 'More of…the situation.' She licked her lips again, hurrying to explain. 'And I'm not afraid. I just…don't know what to do. I know what I said, but…'

Luc's hands relaxed on her shoulders, sliding down her bare arms to leave a wake of goosebumps before he loosely linked her fingers with his own.

'We can simply sit and chat,' he told her gently. 'I enjoyed talking to you.'

'I did too,' Abby admitted. 'That is, talking to you, not to me.'

'Abby.' Luc chuckled softly as he brushed her cheek with his knuckles. 'I understand.'

Abby gave a little nervous laugh. 'You must think me incredibly gauche,' she said and he raised his eyebrows.

'Not at all.'

'Really?' She laughed again, the sound more normal and easy. 'Because, listening to myself, *I* think I sound gauche.' She met his gaze directly, her own gaze open and candid. 'I don't know what to say or do.'

'There's no script, is there?' Luc asked. 'Or did I not get the memo?'

'No script,' Abby confirmed as, still holding her by the hand, he led her to the sofa. 'But surely certain things are…expected?'

'Abby, I promise you, I have no expectations. I was amazed to see you in the bar, and I'm even more amazed to see you here.'

They were sitting on the sofa now, Luc's thigh nearly pressed against her own. Abby slipped off her heels and tucked her stocking-clad feet under the silken folds of her gown.

'Anyway,' Luc continued, 'I don't think you gauche at all. Refreshing, I would have put it.'

'Isn't that just a nice way of meaning "different"?'

'Different is good.'

'Different means different,' Abby insisted. 'Abnormal, weird.'

Luc reached out to touch her ankle through the folds of her gown. It was an almost absent-minded caress, his long, lean fingers lingering on the delicate bones even as his eyes, and his smile, never left her face. 'Is that how you've felt?'

'Sometimes.' Why, Abby wondered, was it so easy to talk to him like this? To admit, confess things, she never had before even to herself? 'Piano was pretty much my life from about age five,' she elaborated with a shrug. 'I stood out.'

'At school?'

She shook her head. 'Not really. I was home-tutored from age eight so I could devote more time to music.'

'Those kids on Hampstead Heath, then?' Luc guessed, and Abby wondered how he knew so much so quickly. *'Them?'*

'Yes,' she agreed wryly. 'Them.'

In the ensuing silence Abby felt herself staring at his leg, at the taut muscle underneath the dark wool, as if fascinated by that one limb, and in truth she was. She wanted to touch it. Him. Wanted to feel the hard muscle underneath, to slide her hand along his hot skin…

What was she thinking? Feeling? Whatever it was, it coursed through her, electric and magical, as he'd described

it. It made her breathless, heady and shy, even as her hand
lifted almost of its own accord, her body emboldened even if
her mind was not.

Her eyes flew to Luc's face. He was smiling at her, too
much knowledge glinting in his own eyes. He reached out and
stroked her cheek with one finger, and Abby could barely keep
from shuddering. She found herself leaning in to that little
caress, openly, wantonly, until her cheek was cupped in Luc's
hand.

He hesitated, and Abby saw the concern and doubt flicker
across his face. She closed her eyes to it, not wanting this
moment to end. She wanted it to go on for ever, to stretch it
out and savour each precious second.

'Abby…' His voice came out as a breath, a plea. Abby's
only response was to turn her head so her lips brushed his
palm. She acted on instinct, on need, knowing this was
foreign territory, frightening and dangerous, yet exciting and
wonderful too. How could she *feel* so much? She felt as if
she'd been numb all her life and was only now melting into
emotion, springing into vitality.

Luc leaned forward and kissed her, his lips softly brushing
hers. Abby's breath hitched at the contact. Twenty-four years
old and she'd never been kissed before—not properly,
anyway. She'd had her fair share of air kisses, the European
double-cheek kiss and some perfunctory pecks. It was all
part of the entertainment business.

But this…this was wonderful. And she wanted more. She
deepened the kiss, surprising herself, and perhaps Luc as
well. She was untouched, unschooled, but need was the best
teacher and it drove her to open her mouth, to touch her
tongue lightly to his; his other hand came up to cradle her face
as his tongue began its own exploration, and Abby felt herself
spinning, her breathing grew ragged, her heart racing as it
never had before.

She heard Luc's breath hitch as well and felt a sharp thrill at the thought that perhaps he was as affected as she was by what was undoubtedly a small, ordinary kiss for most people. Except right now nothing felt small or ordinary; it felt big and special, and wonderfully exciting and new.

Her hands bunched on his shirt, her fingernails snagging on the buttons before she smoothed her palms out, felt the muscles of his chest leap and jerk under her hands. Luc's lips trailed along her jawbone, and then he lowered his head to press a kiss to the silken curve of her neck, dropping lower to her collarbone, and then lower still to the soft swell of her breast above her evening gown.

Abby gasped. She'd never been touched so much, felt so much. *Wanted* so much. Luc's hair, soft and springy, brushed her lips as he continued his path of kisses. Driven by instinct, Abby arched backwards to allow him more access, her mind still spinning, her body lazy and languorous and yet so *alive*… And then it stopped.

He lifted his head, leaving her skin suddenly cool. One of her dress's diamanté straps had slipped off her shoulder, and, smiling wryly, Luc righted it.

'You should go home, Abby.'

Abby started; she was not expecting this, not wanting it. She felt a crushing sense of disappointment she'd hardly thought possible. 'But…why?' Her voice sounded lost and forlorn, and Abby saw an answering bleakness flicker in Luc's eyes.

'Because I don't want to take advantage of you. You're young and innocent, and you should stay that way.'

A white-hot flame of rage blazed through her. 'I'm not a china doll to be kept on a shelf and left alone.'

'I didn't—'

'That's how everyone sees me, Luc. How everyone treats me.' Abby swallowed convulsively, suddenly ridiculously near to tears. She needed Luc to understand this; she wanted to be understood for once. 'Someone to be admired—petted, perhaps, but not touched. Not—' She stopped abruptly, yet her mouth still formed the word silently… *Loved.* 'You're not taking advantage of me if I say yes,' she whispered.

Luc shook his head. 'Do you even know what you're saying yes to?'

Abby gave a shaky little laugh. 'I'm not *that* innocent.'

He brushed a tendril of hair away from her face, his fingertips grazing her cheek. 'If I didn't want you so much,' he murmured, and with sudden boldness Abby took his fingers and pressed them to her mouth.

'I want to be wanted.'

'By me?' he asked, and he sounded both honoured and incredulous.

Abby smiled against his fingers. 'Yes, by you. Only you. I've never…' She paused, for there were too many 'nevers' about this situation. 'Don't ask me to go home,' she said simply. 'Let me stay.'

Luc's eyes darkened, his mouth tightening. 'I'm a selfish man for keeping you here,' he told her in a low voice. 'But, God help me, I will. I don't want to let you go. Not now. Not yet.' His voice turned ragged as he added, half to himself, 'I can't.'

'Then don't,' Abby replied, and her heart finished silently, '*ever*'.

Silently Luc took her by the hand and led her to the bedroom with its sumptuous king-sized bed. She stood there, still and straight, as he slipped the gown from her shoulders, letting it pool on the floor in a dark puddle of silk. Almost reverently he removed her underwear, and Abby thrilled his touch, and at the fact that she wasn't nervous or even embarrassed. How could you be embarrassed by someone who looked at you as if you were the Venus de Milo or the Mona Lisa—an exquisite, priceless treasure?

For that was how Luc looked at her, how he touched her. His fingers barely skimmed her skin, and his head bowed almost reverently. When she was naked he brought her to the bed, and Abby stretched out on the cool sheets, expectant, and now just a little shy.

Luc undressed himself, and she watched as his shed clothes revealed a body of tanned skin and taut muscle. Naked, he stretched out next to her and let his fingers brush her navel. She shivered.

'Cold?'

'No,' she confessed, and he smiled and touched her lips where his hand had been, so Abby shivered again.

'I will do my best not to hurt you,' he murmured, his head still bent, and Abby lightly touched his hair.

'Don't worry,' she said, a new confidence blooming through her. 'You won't hurt me.'

And it didn't hurt. It all felt wonderful, and even more so as Luc touched her, his hands skimming over her body, lips following; every sensation was sharp and exquisite. When Luc let her touch him Abby found herself becoming bold, touching and tasting him as he had her, revelling in his gasps and moans of pleasure.

They didn't speak any longer, but the lack of words didn't bother Abby, for surely this ran too deep for words? What need was there to speak of when their bodies communicated so beautifully, working together in silent, sensuous harmony?

And then it stopped. Luc rolled away, leaving Abby bereft, her arms empty and wanting.

'Luc…' she said, half-gasp, half-moan.

'I don't have protection.' Luc sat on the edge of the bed, his back to her, and ran a shaky hand through his hair. 'To think how close…'

Abby's body ached and throbbed with unfulfilled desire. She moved restlessly on the sheets, her fingers bunching against the rich satin, needing more even though she wasn't entirely sure what 'more' would feel like. 'You aren't going to…?'

'I'll be back in a moment.' Luc gave her a fleeting smile even as he pulled on his clothes. 'We need protection, Abby. I won't play roulette with your life.' He paused, his brows drawing together. 'That is, you don't have protection already? You're not on the Pill?'

Abby shook her head, still dazed with desire. She hadn't even given a thought to birth control or the implications of what they were about to do.

'I'll be back in a moment.'

It felt like it would be a lifetime. With a little smile Abby saw he'd buttoned his shirt wrong; his fingers had been shaking. He pressed a kiss to her damp brow. Abby reached up and touched his jaw, her fingers sliding to his cheek.

'Hurry,' she said, and after a second's pause Luc nodded. 'I will.'

Luc left the room; in the distance Abby heard the soft ping announce the lift's arrival, and then the swoosh of the doors opening and closing. Already she felt horribly alone.

The air felt cold on her naked skin and she wrapped the sheet around her, curling into it, desperate for Luc to return. The events of the evening—the champagne, the rich food and the overwhelming emotion—all caused her to suddenly feel exhausted. Without meaning to or even realizing what she was doing, her eyelids slowly drooped shut.

It was a matter of minutes to find the nearest chemist and buy the necessary items. Back in the suite, Luc strode to the bedroom, his whole body tingling with emotion, awareness. He felt so alive.

He stopped short at the sight of Abby lying in bed, her hair spread like dark silk across the pillow, her lashes fanning her cheek. Her mouth, still swollen from his kisses, was pursed slightly in sleep, and he wondered what she was dreaming about.

Him?

Surely that *was* a dream?

In that moment, the condoms still clenched in his hand, Luc realized with cold, stark clarity how impossible this evening was. How fantastical.

Is this real? Tonight is as real as anything is.

Except, Luc acknowledged as he gazed down at Abby, this wasn't real. He'd lied. This was but a moment in time, an evening taken from reality. And it had to stop now. He'd been about to take her innocence, Luc thought, the realization lashing him. He'd been about to take what wasn't his, selfishly, utterly, and then walk away in the morning, for he knew he had no other choice. He had nothing more to give, nothing more to feel. Already he felt the numbness creep over him once more, his mind, soul and even heart turning cold and blank again.

He was so used to the sensation, it was almost comforting, and only the knowledge of how he might have hurt Abby pierced it like a well-aimed arrow. For surely he would hurt her? Unless…

Unless he left now, before he claimed her for his own and took her innocence. If he left now, while she slept, he would hurt her, but not as much. Not as deeply.

Luc let out a ragged sound, half-sigh, half-cry. He didn't want to go. He wanted nothing more than to lose himself in Abby's embrace for a few hours.

What a selfish bastard he truly was, and always had been, turning a blind eye to another's pain as he took and did what he wanted.

No longer. Slowly, aching with regret and loss for what he'd never really had, Luc slid the unused pack of condoms into his pocket. He reached down to kiss Abby's forehead once more, letting his lips barely brush her skin. She let out a little sigh, and the tiny sound clawed at Luc's heart, causing little shocks of emotion that penetrated the hard shell he'd surrounded himself with. He'd kept himself numb for so long, he hadn't thought he could feel again. He didn't want to. Didn't want to feel the guilt and regret his own failure caused streaming hotly through him.

He'd failed Suzanne. He'd failed her spectacularly, through month after month of never seeing, never understanding. Never doing anything to save her. He wouldn't fail anyone else again, especially not someone as innocent and sweet as Abby. He wouldn't allow himself the opportunity.

She had her life, her music, a whole, wonderful world that had nothing to do with him. It was better that way.

Gently Luc tucked a tendril of hair behind her ear, and let his fingers linger on her cheek before he forced his hand away.

He walked slowly to the doorway, his heart aching, *feeling*. He forced the emotion away, let the numbness settle over him once more like a mantle, a shroud. His coat draped over one arm, he turned back towards her sleeping form and whispered a single word: 'Goodbye.'

Then he stole from the room, so quietly that in her sleep Abby didn't even stir.

CHAPTER FOUR

ABBY woke slowly, languorously, a sleepy warmth still spread over her like a blanket.

'Excusez-moi…'

Abby jerked upright, shock drenching her in icy ripples. A maid stood at the foot of the bed, her eyes downcast, a duster held in one hand.

Abby clutched the sheet to her chest—her naked chest. She didn't have a stitch on; she looked around with a gnawing desperation for Luc. He was nowhere to be seen.

He was gone.

She felt it, just as she'd felt the connection—electric, magical—between them last night. This felt much worse—a consuming emptiness that told her he'd left like a thief in the night, before they'd even… She bit back the thought and its accompanying sob. She didn't need to look down at the floor to see only her clothes strewn there, so carelessly, so obviously, to know he was gone. His departure echoed emptily inside her.

She glanced back at the maid who had raised her eyes to gaze at her with sly speculation that made Abby's whole body flush. From somewhere she dredged the last remaining shreds of her dignity and stared haughtily at the maid.

'Vous pouvez retourner dans quelques minutes…'

The maid nodded and disappeared from the room. Abby heard the lift doors swoosh open and knew she was alone.

Completely alone.

She choked back the sudden grief that threatened to swamp her. Why had he left? He'd gone to buy birth control, for heaven's sake, and then he'd just left her here—why? Had he had second thoughts? Decided she wasn't worth the effort? Would he ever be back? This was his room, after all; perhaps he would return. Surely…?

Abby slipped from the bed, wrapping the sheet more firmly around her as she stalked through the suite looking for clues, promises that he would be back, that he'd just slipped out for coffee.

But of course he hadn't. In a place like this, coffee would have been delivered, along with warm croissants and the newspaper. She and Luc would have lounged in bed, drinking coffee and feeding each other croissants while they shared interesting bits of news they'd read. Then they would have made love as they'd meant to, had been about to, last night, slowly, languorously, taking their time…

Except of course they wouldn't, now, because he was gone. It was a fantasy, just as last night had been a fantasy. What she'd felt had been a fantasy.

False.

Fairy tales didn't happen. They were lies masked as bedtime stories, and she'd been a fool to believe in them—in him—for one moment.

Abby walked through the living room where they'd sat and talked, looking for—what? A scribbled message, a scrap of paper, anything to show her he hadn't left so abruptly, hadn't snuck out while she'd been sleeping with false promises of his quick return. Anything to show her last night had been real, that he'd felt as she had.

There was nothing.

Luc had taken every shred of evidence with him, as thoroughly and mercilessly as a criminal erasing his clues. The bureaux were empty, the cupboards bare.

He was utterly, utterly gone.

Still wrapped in a sheet, Abby sank on the edge of the bed, her mind spinning, desolation skirting on the fringes of her mind.

She couldn't break down, not here, not now.

Not yet.

She took a deep breath and willed herself to think clearly. He was gone; she needed to accept that. She needed to get out of here.

She glanced down at her evening gown, still lying on the floor in a pooled heap of silk. That was all she had to wear, and the thought of walking through the lobby of the hotel in last night's clothes made a fresh flush creep across her body once more as her head bowed in shame.

How could he have done this, have left her? After *everything*? And yet nothing. She'd been aching with desire, her body desperate to join with his, and he'd simply walked away! She closed her eyes, remembering the sweet, sweet pleasure of his hands on her body. A choked sob escaped her and she pressed a trembling fist to her lips. No, she wouldn't think of that. She couldn't, if she wanted to get out of here. She needed strength for the journey home, for surely her father was waiting for her, worried, furious, needing explanations.

What had she done?

Last night she hadn't been thinking of repercussions. She hadn't been thinking at all. She'd just *wanted*, wanted Luc, had wanted the night with him never to end.

And now it had. It had ended hours ago, and she hadn't even realized.

With shaking hands, Abby dressed herself. Her Cinderella's ballgown felt like rags now and left her just as bare. She shrugged on her coat and slipped her feet into the heels. A glance in the mirror showed her pale face, made strained and gaunt by the morning's realizations. The evening gown spoke volumes about how she'd spent her night.

Abby heard the lift doors open once more and knew the maid had returned. She took a deep breath and kept her head held high as she swept towards the foyer.

'*Excusez-moi, mademoiselle,*' the maid murmured. 'The gentleman checked out late last night. I did not realize he had a visitor.'

'I was just leaving,' Abby said in a cold voice, for her pride was all she had right now. Without looking at the maid, unable to bear seeing her scorn or pity, she entered the lift. As the doors closed, she sagged against the bench, the howl of misery inside her threatening to claw right up her throat and spill out in an endless rush of tears.

Somehow she managed to hold it together as she left the hotel. An almost comforting numbness stole over her as she walked alone through the opulent lobby, her head held high, looking neither left nor right. She heard the speculative murmurs in her wake, and knew she'd been recognized. She pushed the thought away, emerging into the street, the crisp morning air cooling her heated cheeks.

She hailed a taxi, relief pouring through her when one pulled up smoothly to the kerb seconds later. She slipped inside, gave her address and closed her eyes.

She'd almost fallen into a doze—sleep was the ultimate an-aesthetic—when the door of the taxi was yanked open.

'Where,' Andrew Summers hissed through clenched teeth, 'have you been?'

Abby paid the driver and slipped out of the taxi. 'I was out,' she said, her voice flat and expressionless. 'Please, Dad, let's not make a scene here.'

Andrew nodded jerkily, and Abby followed him up to their hotel suite.

She stood in the doorway of the small parlour that separated their bedrooms, clutching her jacket to her as her father yanked a miniature bottle of whisky from the room's fridge and unscrewed the cap. He downed it in one angry swallow, surprising Abby, for she'd never known him to drink more than a glass of wine with dinner.

'I had reporters sniffing around here earlier this morning,' he told her, his back to her; still she could see his hands shake as he put down the empty bottle. 'Apparently someone saw you last night with a man.'

And she thought they'd been alone; she thought it had been *providential*. Abby smiled cynically at this naïve thought. She'd grown up a lot in the last twenty-four hours.

'I was,' she confirmed coolly, and her father turned around, his eyebrows raised in disbelief.

'A stranger? You were out with a stranger? Abby, how could you?'

She shrugged, not wanting to admit how easily she could, and had. 'I simply had dinner in a hotel bar. Is that so shocking?'

'The reporters are saying you went upstairs with him,' Andrew stated flatly.

Abby lifted her chin. 'My private life is no one's concern but my own.'

'That's not true,' Andrew returned. 'Your private life is my concern, and the public's concern, because you're a public figure. We've worked hard to make you into a celebrity.'

'Maybe I don't want to be a celebrity.'

Andrew shook his head. 'It's too late for that.'

It was too late for a lot of things, Abby thought wearily. Too late for regrets. She thought of Luc's wish to turn back time. Would she have turned back time if she could, wished last night into never having been?

With a fresh wave of sorrow she realized she wouldn't have. She'd have wished it into *completion*—which must make her truly pathetic. Despite the disappointment of this morning, last night had been magical—for a time. She was glad to have had it, even if it meant facing this morning and its harsh realities alone.

'I need to shower,' she told her father. 'And change. After that we can talk.' She saw surprise flicker across his face and knew he wasn't used to her giving orders. She wasn't used to it, either, but without another word she left the parlour in a swirl of silk and closed the door of her bedroom.

In her *en suite* bathroom she turned the shower on full blast and stripped the gown from her body, kicking it into a corner on the floor. She never wanted to see or wear it again; it felt tainted. Everything did.

She stepped into the shower and let the scalding water stream over her like tears. The beauty of last night, she realized, the promise and the potential, did not make up for the ugliness of this morning. Why had Luc left so suddenly, without a word of explanation or farewell?

The answer was obvious—he didn't want to be found. For whatever reason he'd changed his mind about being with her, and hadn't wanted the confrontation of telling her so. Abby closed her eyes. Was she so undesirable, so gauche in the bedroom that he'd been able to leave in the middle of their encounter? She gave a little laugh of disbelief. Honestly, if he'd been able to leave so easily, she didn't have what it would have taken to make him stay.

Once she was dressed and showered, she returned to the parlour, where her father sat on the sofa, his mobile phone clenched to one ear. The expression on his face was grim, and almost idly Abby wondered to whom he was talking. The concert-hall manager? A reporter? Her agent?

He snapped the phone shut and swivelled to look at Abby. 'That was your mother.'

She felt a faint flicker of surprise; as first violinist of an orchestra in Manchester, her mother had a busy schedule, and rarely rang while Abby was on tour.

'Is everything all right?'

'No, Abigail,' her father replied tersely, 'everything is *not* all right. Your mother read in the paper this morning about the Piano Prodigy's mystery man!'

The Piano Prodigy; it was how she'd been marketed since she'd started playing professionally at age seventeen. And, while she'd never particularly liked it, right now the words seemed so cold, so inhuman. Abby walked to the window, twisting a damp strand of hair around her finger as she gazed out at the city landscape of early spring. The trees lined the boulevard, still stark and bare against a dank, grey sky.

'I don't think,' Andrew continued in that same tight voice, 'you realize what last night meant.'

A harsh bark of laughter escaped her. 'I know exactly what it meant.' *Nothing.*

'For your career,' Andrew emphasized. 'Although also…' he trailed off, and Abby could only imagine the questions he was unable to ask.

Although her father had been both her manager and mentor for years, they'd never had the kind of relationship that encouraged personal revelation or intimacy. Abby still remembered getting her period in the middle of a piano lesson. She'd asked the mother of another pupil what to do, and kindly the woman had run out and got the necessary items at a nearby chemist. The woman had also told her father, who had looked stricken. They'd never spoken about it, of course, just as they wouldn't speak of this. Abby wasn't a woman, or even a daughter—she was a pianist. A prodigy.

'Why should it mean anything to my career?' she asked

now, although the question had little interest for her. At that moment, her career hardly mattered.

'It doesn't help your image to be known as a party girl,' Andrew said after a moment.

'A party girl?' Abby turned around. 'A *party girl*?' she repeated in disbelief. Her life was so far from that—from either the party or the girl. She'd never done anything, *anything* that earned such a statement, such a judgement…until last night.

Last night she'd thrown everything to the winds—her reputation, her career, her life—in order to spend an evening with a man. A man who wanted nothing more to do with her, who hadn't even wanted her enough in the first place.

'Abigail,' Andrew said in a voice of strained patience. 'We have worked very hard to get where we are now. We've guarded your reputation, nurtured it as a woman of singular devotion and talent.'

Abby didn't miss the use of the plural pronoun '*we*'. Everything she'd done, her father felt *he'd* done. It had always been so. Her career was a joint enterprise, and her father had just as much, or perhaps far more, invested in it as she did. He felt any rumour or speculation, any threat, keenly.

Yet he didn't feel the betrayal of last night.

Only she felt that.

Abby turned back to the window and gazed once more at the bleak boulevard. A light, misting drizzle had begun to fall once more. She stiffened in surprise when she felt her father's hand on her shoulder.

'Abby—whatever happened last night…' Her father trailed off, and Abby knew that was the best he could manage. It was his brand of sympathy, and from somewhere she dredged up a smile.

'It's all right.'

'You'll just have to play your heart out tonight,' Andrew continued briskly. 'A stellar performance erases all sins.'

Sins. An apt word, Abby thought, and somehow she managed to nod, as if she were agreeing with him.

She didn't play her heart out that night; perhaps she had no more heart. She felt cold and numb, and in fact she didn't play very well at all. She stumbled during the *Apassionata* badly enough for people to notice, and she heard the collective little gasp. She didn't even care. She continued playing, vaguely aware that the music was as flat as her feelings, her heart. Numb, lifeless.

At the intermission her father, waiting in the wings, tensely told her to relax. Abby could see the worry in his eyes, and she wondered if it was for herself or her career. Had there been any self? she wondered now, gazing in the mirror at her own pale, drawn face. Or had there simply been the music?

Always the music, her father's joy and passion. But had it been hers? For the first time in twenty-four years, Abby felt like answering 'no', and the realization made a wave of fresh sorrow break over her and recede so that only the numbness was left.

The second half of the concert was as listless and unfocused as the first. No one came back with the requests for autographs her father would deny; no one came back at all. Perhaps they were confused. Perhaps they didn't care.

In any case, Abby and her father remained alone backstage, Abby changing while her father paced outside her dressing room, talking tersely on his mobile to her agent.

'Isn't the saying "no publicity is bad publicity"? I *know*, Randall, but this will pass... We have six concerts left on this tour... She can do it.'

But I can't do it, Abby thought suddenly as she stared in the mirror and listened to her father's increasingly desperate pleas. *And, even if I could, I don't want to.* For twenty-four years she'd lived for the music. Now she wanted to live for herself.

When Abby came out of the dressing room, Andrew was slipping the phone into his pocket. He gave her a tired smile. 'I know tonight wasn't the best we've ever played, Abby, but we have a couple of days until we need to be in Milan, and I think we both could use a rest.'

We, Abby thought, always *we*. As a girl it had made her feel special, included, part of something bigger than herself. Now it both irritated and saddened her. She knew the bare bones of her father's story: he'd been a pianist too, but his talent hadn't got him far, or not far enough, so he'd poured his creative energy into her instead. And she didn't have any more room for it.

'I want to cancel the rest of the tour,' she said quietly. 'I'm…burned out. I need more than a few days' rest.'

Andrew stared at her for a long moment, his mouth dropping open in shock. 'Abby—'

'We can refund the money if we need to,' Abby continued, her voice becoming firmer, more certain. This was what she needed, what she craved. Her night with Luc had merely been the wake-up call. 'I've been playing and recording non-stop for seven years. I need a break. A big one.'

Andrew let out a shaky breath. 'All right,' he said after a moment. 'All right. But after this tour—'

'I can't,' Abby replied simply. 'You heard me tonight. I can't. We can refund—'

'No,' Andrew cut her off, and he sounded angry for the first time. 'We can't.'

Abby stared at him, felt the first fingers of dread creep along her spine. Finally, after a long moment, she asked in a level voice, 'Why not?'

'Because I lost it, Abby.' Sorrow replaced anger, and her father hung his head. 'I lost it all.'

CHAPTER FIVE

Six months later

SITTING in the warm September sunshine in a street café in Avignon, Luc gazed at the column of print, no more than a side item in the arts section of *Le Monde: Piano Prodigy Abigail Summers retires.*

Luc felt a lurch deep in his gut. It was guilt, he knew, the guilt he'd tried to keep at bay now roiling through him. He'd tried not to think of Abby or that one wonderful yet unfulfilled night six months ago. He'd tried to forget her, for her own sake. She didn't need him in her life. She *couldn't*. So he'd stayed blank, cold, numb, as always, and immersed himself in work so there was no one left to hurt.

Yet as he stared at the fine print, accompanied by a rather grainy photo of Abby playing in some anonymous concert hall, he knew he hadn't forgotten her. At all. He might not have been actively thinking of her, but she'd been present in his mind, in his thoughts. In his memory.

And now he felt the guilt deepen and intensify within him, turning into a solid mass of anxiety that lodged in his middle and clawed its way up his throat. Why had she retired?

Was it because of me?

Had he hurt another innocent with his greed, his need,

despite his intentions otherwise? He shouldn't have spoken to her, or ordered champagne, dinner and the suite… There had been a dozen different opportunities to stop, to turn away, to keep himself from hurting her. He hadn't taken any of them.

'*Salut*, Luc.'

Luc looked up from the newspaper to see his solicitor, Denis Depaul, coming towards him. He tossed the paper aside, wishing he could discard his memories and concerns as easily.

'*Salut,*' he replied.

Denis sat down and ordered a coffee before he continued speaking. 'It is good to see you. I thought I might not have the opportunity; you have been working so hard.' He paused. 'And you come down south so rarely these days.'

'Yes.' He spoke in a clipped voice, then forced himself to relax and smile. Denis was an old family friend; he'd served his father before his death when Luc was only eleven, and had protected and nurtured the family assets as best he could until Luc had been old enough to take the reins of Toussaint Holdings.

Luc would never forget those desperate years, when Toussaint Holdings had slid and slipped quietly, inch by inch, franc by franc, into total financial disaster, beset by corruption and crooked managers. Denis had done the best he could while Luc had watched, irate, incapable, and only twelve years old.

'I have news.'

Luc took a sip of his espresso. 'Oh?' he asked, his voice neutral.

'Yes.' Denis paused. 'There has been an offer on Chateau Mirabeau.'

Luc stilled, his fingers curled around his tiny cup of coffee. 'An offer?' he repeated in the same neutral tone. 'I did not realize it was for sale.'

'Of course it is not, but it has been shut up like a box for six months; people begin to wonder.'

'Let them wonder.' Luc's voice was flat, ominously so, but Denis was not deterred.

'It is quite a good offer, Luc. Of course you don't need the money, but considering—'

'Considering?' Luc repeated. 'Considering what?'

Denis paused for only a moment, his head cocked to one side. There was something too close to pity in his eyes, Luc thought. 'Considering,' he replied evenly, 'that you no longer live there, and have expressed no interest in living there in the future.' He leaned forward, his expression turning compassionate—too compassionate; Luc found he could not bear it. He surely did not deserve it. He didn't want sympathy, or even understanding.

It would have been easier if Denis had condemned him, blamed him as no one ever had for Suzanne's death, even though his own mind and heart were weighed down with guilt. *If I'd paid attention… If I'd loved her… If I'd realized how desperate and unhappy I'd made her…*

Perhaps she would still be alive.

'Luc, it is a good offer. And the chateau, with its memories…' He trailed off, but Luc could have filled in what he hadn't said.

He knew all about memories: Chateau Mirabeau, with its stone terraces and vineyards, its fountains and aquaducts, its secrets, sorrows and scars. Chateau Mirabeau, where Suzanne had lived so unhappily and died so suddenly.

'I can't sell it,' Luc said, his voice uncompromising. 'It has been in our family for four hundred years. My father—' He stopped abruptly, his throat tight, and simply shook his head.

'I know your father would not have wished such a thing to come to pass,' Denis said gently. 'But neither could he have ever imagined such circumstances as these. Selling the chateau might help, Luc, and I don't mean just your bank account. You need to—'

'It's not your job to tell me what I need,' Luc cut him off coldly. 'Save for matters concerning my bank accounts.' He knew he sounded curt, but he didn't apologize. He didn't want advice; he didn't even want kindness. He looked away, and jerked slightly when Denis laid a hand over his arm, removing it after a brief moment and shrugging philosophically. 'As you wish. Thirty-five million pounds might change your mind, however.'

'Thirty-five million?' Luc arched an eyebrow, equanimity restored, or at least appearing to be. 'That's all?'

Denis gave a little chuckle. 'I told you, you don't need it. But still, in these times, thirty-five million pounds is thirty-five million pounds.'

'No.'

Denis shrugged again. 'As I said before, as you wish.' He took a folder out of his attaché case and began to discuss Luc's other assets in the Languedoc, but Luc found his mind wandering. Once a conversation such as this would have been meat and drink to him: ways to preserve his family's heritage, increase its revenue, restore its name. He still worked hard to keep Toussaint Holdings profitable, but he didn't let himself think about it. He concentrated on numbers, figures, bank balances and ledgers, and refused to think about what lay behind them: the dusty vineyards, the ancient walls, the twisted olive groves and orange trees, the house and land that he'd loved too much.

As Denis spoke he found his glance slipping back to the paper, to the grainy photograph of 'Piano Prodigy Abigail Summers'.

Abby.

Again he felt guilt roil through him. Six months ago she'd been at the pinnacle of her career, or close to it. She'd had everything she could ever possibly want—and now she'd retired? Just like that?

Why?

The answer seemed, felt, obvious: because of him. Because he'd taken too much from her and then slipped out of her life without a single word of explanation, without even a goodbye.

He'd convinced himself it had been better that way. If he'd waited, he would have crumbled. He would have taken her in his arms and made love to her; he wouldn't have let her go. Not then, not yet.

And then what? She would have become more attached, more involved; perhaps she would have even imagined she loved him. And he would have hurt her, disappointed her, *failed* her, eventually. Just as he had Suzanne.

Still, Luc thought not for the first time, he could have softened the blow. Explained…something.

'Luc?' Luc jerked his unfocused gaze back to his solicitor, who tapped a sheaf of papers with a gold-plated pen. 'Just going over the winery profits.'

'Yes, of course,' Luc said, although he had no idea what Denis had been saying. He forced himself to concentrate, but even so his mind slipped back not only to the article in the newspaper but to that night, to Abby herself.

He remembered how she'd felt against him; she'd fit perfectly. He could still recall how her hair had had such a soft, flowery fragrance, like lavender. It had reminded him of home, in a good way, which was strange. Amazing, really. When he'd held her in his arms, the ghosts had left him. He hadn't heard their mocking voices; the memories hadn't claimed him. He'd been at peace.

'Luc?' Denis prompted again, and Luc nodded.

'I'm here.'

But he wasn't here. Already his mind was miles away, thinking of where Abby could have gone…and how he could find her.

Abby slipped the home-cooked lasagne out of the industrial freezer and added it to the box of food on the counter.

'Anything else going to Corner Cottage?' she asked Grace Myer, her boss for the last four months and owner of Cornish Country Kitchen Catering.

Grace tucked a flyaway strand of greying hair behind her ear and consulted the order. 'Lasagne, salad, bread and an apple crumble. I think that's it. It's just for the one man.'

'He's here for the week?'

'Yes. He only rented the property a few days ago. Must have been a last-minute thing.' She laid the order form on top of the box. 'There you go. You're all right to go to Helston this afternoon?'

Abby nodded. 'No problem.' Part of the reason Grace had hired her was to do the toing and froing, the heavy work that she couldn't manage with an increasingly bad back. Abby was glad to do it, glad, actually, to be useful, to keep herself busy and productive in a way she never had been before. It helped to be busy; then she didn't have quite so much time to think.

Now she hefted the box and headed out of the thatched cottage from where Grace ran her business supplying self-catering cottages with ready meals. The September day was crisp and sunny with a light breeze blowing in from the sea ruffling Abby's hair.

She loaded the box in the back of Grace's old van and then climbed in the driver's side. The sea was a bright-blue ribbon along her right-hand side, the sky a lighter blue above her as she drove down the coast road to Carack, the little fishing village where Corner Cottage was located.

It occurred to her, not for the first time, how much her life had changed in the last six months. That night in Paris, her father's revelation that their—*her*—assets had vanished completely, had been the turning point of both her life and career. She'd played two more concerts, played badly, before cancelling the rest of the tour. In a wave of speculative concern and spurious interest, she'd left the music scene, left every despised remnant of the life she'd known. And now she was here.

She spent most of her days driving to and from various self-catering cottages with boxes of meals. The mundane nature of her work was alleviated by the sight of the sea and sky, the occasional trips to Helston or Penzance for supplies and the friends she'd made—whether it was Marta, the older woman who had been running Carack's tiny shop, 'the Harrods of Cornwall', for thirty years, the postman, or Grace herself. Small, simple pleasures, ones she'd come to savour.

It had been an instinctive decision to come to Cornwall, one she hadn't really needed to think about. She'd gone on holiday here as a child, when her mother had played a music festival in Devon. It had been a glorious week of building sandcastles and eating melting ice-creams, one of the few holidays she'd had with her family *as* a family. It felt good to be back. She didn't regret it, or her decision to answer Grace's tiny ad in the local paper for an assistant. Her parents had been bewildered, the public stunned, and yet Abby was glad. She needed a complete respite, relief from the life she'd known, the person she'd been. The 'Prodigy'.

For the first time in her life—besides that one night with Luc—she felt free. Free and, in small, simple ways, happy.

Yet just the thought of Luc caused a little pang of sorrow to shoot through her like a lingering toothache, a sudden, surprising, jagged pain. She'd stopped being angry a few months ago; anger was too exhausting. She didn't know why Luc had left—had he planned to all along? Had he simply lost interest? Did it even matter?

As the anger receded, she found she could even, in an objective way, summon a little surprising gratitude. Luc had woken her up; he'd made her see how limited and caged her life had been, even if he hadn't meant to. Had made her feel.

Still, it hurt. It made her sad to think of what she thought might have been, now knowing it never could have. Yet she was glad for the wake-up call she'd so obviously needed.

'Maybe if I keep telling myself that, I'll believe it,' she said wryly. She'd started talking to herself as she drove the van along the narrow, twisting lanes with hedgerows high on either side. She remembered that night with Luc when she'd spoken aloud to her own reflection. She'd felt lonely then, a bit pathetic, but now she found she liked her little one-way conversations. It reminded her that she'd chosen this. She'd chosen to leave the past behind, to move ahead, to finally live and feel, even if it hurt.

Surely that was better than the numbness she'd first felt after Luc had left? Surely feeling pain along with the joy was better than feeling nothing at all?

Corner Cottage was the last of a row of terraced cottages on the high street of Carack, whitewashed, thatched and facing the sea. The air was cool and sharp with brine as Abby parked the van in front of the cottage and went to unload the box of meals.

She let herself in by the back gate, through a tiny garden, right into the little brick-floored kitchen. She loved Corner Cottage. It was tiny, with just the little kitchen and a parlour that was dominated by a stone fireplace, with a cozy bedroom above, the bed tucked snugly under the eaves. It was one of the area's most popular rentals for couples, and Abby could see why. The sight of the slate-blue sea winking from the bedroom window made you want to curl up in the huge bed with its thick, fluffy duvet and stay there for ever.

Part of Abby's job was to check the cottage was ready for the next tenants, and after unloading the food she went upstairs to make sure the rooms were prepared and clean. Just the sight of that high, wide bed caused a pang of memory to pierce her again, and for a second she let herself imagine being in that bed with Luc. She had no one else to imagine doing such a thing with, as he'd been the sum total of her romantic and sexual experience—limited as it so obviously was. A few men she'd met through the course of her work flirted with her, and one had asked her out for a drink at the local pub.

Abby had gone. Since that morning, after being with Luc when she'd woken up alone, so terrifyingly numb, she had been determined to live life to the fullest, accepting invitations, laughing, dancing or just enjoying life when she could. She hadn't enjoyed that evening. The man, a local carpenter, had been too full of himself and his own importance. Abby had barely managed to get a word in edgeways, and she'd taken herself home alone at nine o'clock.

Now it was all too easy to imagine herself in that bed, to remember how long, lean and perfect Luc's body had been, how cherished she'd felt in his arms. Those moments felt like the most precious and most real of her life. Or was she simply romanticizing her one experience?

Of course she was. The cold, hard fact that he'd walked away before they'd even made love proved that.

'A bit pathetic, really,' Abby said aloud, shaking her head. She needed to stop thinking about Luc; his memory crept up on her in these unexpected moments, made her feel vulnerable. 'What I really need to do,' Abby said, 'is go out on another date. Just not with that carpenter.'

She headed downstairs, only to check herself when she

heard the sound of a key turning in the front door's heavy, old-fashioned lock. The new tenant wasn't supposed to arrive until three, and it was only noon. Shrugging, Abby decided she might as well say hello and confirm that everything was just as it should be.

That friendly, professional smile was already on her face as she stood in the centre of the cozy little parlour, ready to greet whoever opened the door. The words 'welcome to Corner Cottage' were in her mouth, about to trip off her tongue.

Then the door opened, and the words died as the smile slid off her face. She was staring right at Luc.

CHAPTER SIX

SHE looked so much the same, Luc thought, the key still in his hand as he stood there gazing at her motionless, transfixed, drinking her in like a man dying of thirst.

She didn't move either; her own mouth was open in shock, her face pale, her eyes wide. So much the same…and yet so different. Her dark, glossy hair was caught up in a careless ponytail, and instead of an evening gown she worn jeans and a red parka over a cotton tee-shirt. She looked as fresh and scrubbed as any village girl, and yet she had a lifetime of cosmopolitan experience. He'd reduced her to this, to menial work for a second-rate catering company. Guilt sliced through him once more, and made him take a step into the room and slide the heavy key into his pocket. 'Hello, Abby.'

She shook her head slowly, a gesture of both disbelief and denial. 'What are you doing here?'

'I…' He paused, wondering how much to say. 'I wanted to see you.'

'You came here on purpose.' It was a statement, not a question; he recognized that for the obvious fact it indeed was. A man like him would hardly visit a tiny cottage in the middle of nowhere for no reason. He would frequent glamorous hotels and resorts, spas and ski lodges—places like Hotel Le

Bristol, Luc thought, a spasm of remembrance shooting through him.

'Yes.'

'To see me,' she clarified, and he heard the incredulity, the latent anger.

'Yes.' He stared at her, struggling to keep his voice even. He hated how stilted he sounded, how he was powerless to keep the memories, the feelings, from rushing back, from overwhelming him with their force. Seeing Abby now made him remember afresh how wonderful that night had been—*could* have been. He swallowed, forcing the feeling back. He couldn't afford regrets, not those kind. Still he stepped closer to her, inhaling her scent. She smelled, he thought, like clean laundry and fresh bread. 'I had a devil of a time finding you,' he continued, his voice steady now. 'But I did, and now I'm here.'

'Why?' Abby crossed her arms, her eyes flashing, her tone turning soft and almost menacing in a way Luc had never heard before.

He paused. 'I needed to make sure you were all right.'

Abby's mind was spinning. She was conscious of so many things—the latent anger that spurted hotly through her now, surprising her, her clammy hands, the heavy thud of her own heart. Most of all, Luc. The way he looked—the strong, surprisingly familiar lines of his cheek and jaw, his hair that still touched his collar, his eyes so piercingly, *achingly* blue, his arms which were held loosely at his sides, making her want to walk straight to him and have him fold her up in an embrace.

Abby took a step back. That wasn't going to happen. 'Let me get this straight,' she finally said, keeping her voice as even as his. 'You needed to salve your conscience by making sure I wasn't heartbroken about the night we *almost* had together over six months ago now—is that about it?'

Two spots of colour appeared high on Luc's cheekbones. Was he actually embarrassed? Abby wondered. Or just angry? She shook her head and spread her arms wide. Her voice trembled a little. 'Consider your conscience salved, Luc. I'm fine.'

He didn't move. 'You retired from piano.'

'A decision that had nothing to do with you.'

Luc's mouth tightened. 'The newspaper said you'd canceled several concerts.'

Abby felt another rush of anger, which surprised her again, for she thought she'd done with this. With him. Perhaps she had, in theory. Yet now Luc stood in front of her, looking all too wonderful, making her realize how much she'd actually missed him, and demanding answers he had no right to know. 'It really isn't your concern, Luc,' she said wearily. 'The lasagne is in the fridge.'

'The lasagne?' Luc exhaled sharply. 'The only reason I ordered meals was to see you!'

'Well, you've seen me.' She gave a humourless little laugh. 'You must have done some detective work to find me here. Even the newspapers don't know where to look, although I suppose I'm old news by now.'

'Why did you leave piano, Abby?'

'I told you, it had nothing to do with you.'

'I find that hard to believe.'

She laughed disbelievingly. 'Would you *prefer* me to be heartbroken?'

Luc's jaw tightened, his eyes narrowing. Was this actually the man she'd almost slept with? Abby wondered. The man she'd believed herself half in love with? She really had been embarrassingly naïve, for the man before her now was cold, disinterested, even dismissive. Was she simply one more problem to solve? Why had he come here at all?

'I just need to know why you left.'

Abby let out a short breath of exasperation. She felt

drained emotionally and physically by the last few minutes, and knew she should just walk out of the door. That would be the smart thing to do.

Yet when it came to this man she'd never been very smart. And the thought of leaving him now caused fresh sorrow to sweep through her in an unbearable wave. Stupidly.

'If you're going to demand answers,' she finally said, keeping her voice brisk and a little wry, 'then I'm going to demand a cup of tea.' She moved past him into the kitchen, filling the kettle with water and plonking it on the stove, the efficient, everyday movements keeping back the tide of emotion and memory. Her body was still weak and tingling from just seeing him, the shock still rippling through her. She'd never thought she'd see him again, and it was only now that he was here that she realized how much she'd wanted to.

'Do you miss it?' Luc asked quietly, and, teapot in hand, Abby stilled. She didn't need to ask what Luc meant. *Do you miss it?* All of it…everything: the glamour, the crowds, the jetting lifestyle. And the music. Most of all, the music.

The music was the hunger in her soul. She'd gone so long that she had forgotten what it felt like to be satisfied, not to feel that endless ache. Carefully she reached for teabags from the jar above the stove and put two in the pot. 'No,' she said finally. 'Not as much as I thought I would, anyway.' Yet she knew she was lying, at least in part. She missed the music. She missed wanting the music, needing it, loving it, having it consume her.

'Why did you retire, Abby?' Luc asked, his voice low and intense as he moved closer to her, filling the small kitchen. 'Why did you leave it all so suddenly?'

'You really have the most amazing guilt complex,' Abby told him. She turned around and found a smile. 'You blame yourself, don't you? You think you ruined my career.'

'It made me wonder,' Luc replied coolly. 'Tell me I'm

wrong.' Although he kept his voice detached, almost cold, Abby heard the sorrow, the grief, underneath. It reminded her of the man he'd been in Paris six months ago—a man who seemed tormented by regret. What had happened to make Luc the man he was, tortured by guilt? What had he done?

'You're wrong, Luc,' she said quietly. 'It wasn't you, not really. It was me.'

'What happened?'

Behind her the kettle whistled and Abby busied herself, making herself at home in the kitchen, preparing tea. She needed the time to sort her thoughts and prepare an answer. *What happened?* So much.

'I suppose a lot of things happened at the same time,' she finally said when the tea was ready. She handed Luc a mug and they stood in silence, hands cradled around their mugs, both of them lost in thought, waiting.

'Our night together was a bit of a wake-up call,' Abby continued after a moment, choosing her words carefully. 'I realized then how closed, how *caged*, my life was. I know it looked glamorous from the outside, but all I've known, all I've ever known, is piano—concert halls and practising and not much else.' She took a sip of tea. 'Not much of a life.'

'And you wanted to change that?' Luc asked eventually.

Abby paused, remembering. She hadn't wanted mere change; she'd wanted escape. The lacklustre reviews had simply spurred her on. She took another sip of tea. 'Yes. And, to be frank, I needed it. I was, as they say in the trade, burned out. And it showed.'

'You're brilliant,' Luc objected and Abby shrugged.

'I stopped being brilliant.' She still felt the sting of the disappointed audiences, the scathing reviews. And worse, far worse, had been the emptiness within herself, the feeling that the intimate connection she'd forged with music had suddenly been severed. It had left her grieving, lost, adrift in a sea of self-imposed silence, and so she'd gone. She was glad…now. At least, she told herself she was.

They both lapsed into silence; the only sound was the distant swoosh of the sea, the endless pull and tug of the tide.

'All right,' Luc finally said. 'But why Cornwall? Why heft boxes like some lackey?'

He didn't keep the disbelieving disdain from his voice, and Abby bristled. 'There's nothing wrong with manual labour.'

'It's beneath you. What if you injured your hands? What if you lost the ability to play?'

Abby had considered this, but when she'd taken the job with Cornish Country Kitchen Catering she'd been too weary and heartsore to care. 'I haven't played piano in six months,' she said quietly. 'I sometimes wonder if I'll ever play again.' She'd never spoken those words, that fear, aloud, and now they tore at her soul. She looked away from Luc's shocked face.

'Don't,' she warned him, trying to laugh, 'take this on yourself. This has very little to do with you, and everything to do with me and my family.'

'Your family?'

'My parents are professional musicians. It's all they've known, all they've ever cared about. Right around the time I was born, my mother's career as a violinist began to take off. My father's career as a pianist was faltering, and so he took over as my primary care-giver.'

She spoke flatly, as if she were talking about someone else. She almost felt like she was; she certainly now felt like a different person from the girl or even the woman she'd been. 'He poured all his love of piano into me, as well as all of his ambition. I never wanted to let him down.' The long days of mindless work here in Cornwall had caused her to relive her own life's history in her mind, making realizations and connections that had never occurred to her before. It hadn't been the most comfortable of times, but it had been good. Necessary.

'That may be,' Luc said eventually. 'But your talent is obvious, and undoubtedly surpasses your father's. That's not something that can be forced.'

'Perhaps not,' Abby agreed. 'But talent and desire don't always go hand in hand. At least, the desire to perform professionally.' Yet to *play*—to feel the music emerge and dance under her fingers—was just as much of a desire and even a need as it had ever been. 'Anyway,' she continued, suddenly feeling restless with the discussion about herself, 'who knows? Perhaps I'll play again, if I'm given the opportunity. By the time I'm ready to go back, the world might have latched on to some *other* piano prodigy.' She made a face as she spoke her own despised nickname.

'I doubt it,' Luc said evenly. 'But if you wanted a break, why not go to a resort or hotel? Have a proper holiday, instead of—'

'Working like some skivvy?' Abby laughed. 'This is like a holiday for me, Luc, of sorts.'

'You certainly have the money—'

'Actually,' she cut him off, 'I don't.' She turned to rinse her mug in the sink. She hadn't meant to divulge that little fact, but Luc somehow had the ability to wring the truth from her, no matter how unpalatable or humiliating. He took a step towards her; she could feel his tension.

'Abby, what do you mean?'

'My father was in charge of investing all my money,' Abby said, her back to him. 'I always had what I needed, and I never thought about it much, frankly. Anyway…' She took a breath, let it out. 'Right around the time I felt burned out—' *the night you left me*, she couldn't help but think '—I discovered he'd lost virtually all the profits from seven years of playing. Risky stock-investments and a downturn in the economy.' She shrugged. 'He's a musician, not a banker.'

Luc swore under his breath. 'What about continued royalties from the albums you've made?'

'There are only two, and, years on, they're not big sellers. It provides a little bit, that's all.'

'You could sue him.'

'Oh, Luc.' Abby turned around, shaking her head. 'Do you think I want revenge? He's my father. Besides, he doesn't have any money to pay for a settlement. I feel sorry for him, to tell you the truth. I think he was more invested in my career than I was.'

'What is he doing now?'

Abby shrugged. Her father had been disgusted by her choice to live in Cornwall and work like some common drudge. They were hardly ever in touch, and the only time he called was to implore her to return to the music scene. 'Probably in London, trying to drum up some work for me. The last offer was playing somewhere in Brighton for pensioners.'

'And what about your mother?'

'She's pursuing her own career. My parents have lived virtually separate lives since I started to tour. She offered to have me come live with her in Manchester, perhaps teach piano to children, but I didn't want that. I needed to make my own life, and I have.' She paused, and when she spoke again there was an edge to her voice. 'I can tell you don't think much of it, but it's mine, and amazingly enough I've been happy here.'

Luc was silent for a long moment. 'If you need money…'

She drew herself up, her breath coming out in a hiss. 'I don't.'

'I won't have you working here like a skivvy simply because—'

'You have no choice, Luc. You have no control over my life.'

Luc's eyes flashed brilliant azure, sharp as iron. He suddenly seemed like a dangerous man, and Abby took a step back, coming up hard against the sink. 'Don't tell me you walked away from it all just because of your father? I had something to do with it, Abby. I set the chain of events in motion.'

'You have an amazing ego,' Abby spat. She trembled with an anger she didn't even understand.

'Do I? Because that night affected me as much as I think it affected you.' His voice turned ragged, his eyes burning into hers, transfixing her. 'Six months on, and I can't even begin to forget. It still haunts me.'

Abby opened her mouth to utter a scathing retort, yet no sound came. Luc's admission rocked her. She wanted to believe it—believe that night hadn't been a lie, believe in the fairy tale, even—but she couldn't. Not when his hasty departure had told otherwise.

'Still,' she finally managed. 'It was six months ago. We've both moved on, Luc. We have nothing now. So…' She drew in a breath, needing courage to make the final cut. 'Why don't you leave me alone now? Go back to Paris, or the Languedoc, or wherever you came from.'

Luc gazed at her, his eyes dark with longing, the only sound the harsh tear of their own breathing. He reached out to touch the inside of her wrist with two fingers, as she'd touched him in the bar when she'd so blatantly offered herself. 'I can't.'

Abby closed her eyes; he was still touching her. Just the feel of his fingers, the sound of his voice—low, with that faint French lilt—made her defences weaken. Crumble.

'Have dinner with me,' Luc said. 'Tonight.'

Abby's heart gave a little jump; shock and something else, fear or hope, or perhaps both. 'I don't think that's a good idea.'

'Probably not,' Luc agreed with a crooked smile that made

Abby's already jumpy heart do a half-turn. 'But have dinner with me anyway.'

'I said yes once before,' Abby told him, 'and I regretted it.' She tried to slip her arm away from him but he held on, his fingers curling around her wrist, his thumb brushing that tender skin that made her whole body quiver with both expectation and remembrance.

'Do you, Abby?' he asked softly. 'Do you regret it?' His eyes met hers, searching, knowing, and Abby could not look away. She couldn't lie, either.

'No,' she said quietly, 'but I should. And, even if I don't regret it, I don't want to repeat it, either.' That *was* a lie, she knew, or at least a half-truth. She pulled her arm away from him, succeeding this time, and found herself cradling the limb as if she were injured. She wasn't, but the memory of his touch hurt her in another way.

'Dinner,' Luc told her, 'that's all.' He waited, his gaze pleading with hers, yet still exuding a male confidence. Damn him; she was so close to saying yes. Because she wanted to see him again. She wanted to touch him again. To have him touch her…even if he slipped away once more, even if he didn't say goodbye.

'No, Luc.' Abby didn't know where she found the strength to refuse; it must have taken every ounce of her energy, for her body sagged with the effort of saying those two little words. 'I'm sorry. It's just…I can't. I *can't*.' She couldn't look at him as she slipped past him and through the door, and by the time she'd reached the gate she was running. Running away.

CHAPTER SEVEN

LUC stood in the doorway of Corner Cottage, watching as Abby hurried down the little brick path, clearly desperate to escape him. And why shouldn't she? She should run as fast as she could, away from him. She'd learned her lesson six months ago; why hadn't he?

He still wanted her.

He'd come to Cornwall with the best of intentions. At least, Luc acknowledged starkly, he'd convinced himself he had good intentions. He wanted to see her, explain why he'd left the way he had if such a thing could be explained. He wanted, as he'd admitted to Abby, to make sure she was all right. *Consider your conscience salved...* Luc winced as he remembered Abby's words. He must have seemed an arrogant, self-centred bastard to come here simply to make himself feel better. She'd seen through him, seen the selfishness that he'd wilfully blinded himself to. He hadn't come for her sake; he'd come for his own.

Why had he asked her out to dinner? He was meant to be leaving her alone, yet he'd pursued her with an urgent desire than was utterly selfish. He *still* couldn't let her go.

Luc cursed aloud.

He couldn't leave it at this. He wouldn't leave Abby like this, whether she wanted him to or not. She deserved more,

more than he could ever give, but he could at least see her provided for. Make sure she was all right financially and physically, if not emotionally.

Even as he made these resolutions, Luc wondered if he was blinding himself once more, wilfully turning away from the truth: that he simply wanted, needed, to see her again, and this was merely his excuse.

'You don't look so good.'

Abby winced wryly. 'I had trouble sleeping last night,' she admitted as she came into the kitchen of Grace's cottage.

'Any particular reason why?' Grace asked lightly. She moved around the airy space, opening the oven to check on a batch of cinnamon buns. Abby inhaled their sweet, yeasty fragrance.

'Not really,' she prevaricated. Actually, there was a very particular reason why: Luc. From the moment she'd left Corner Cottage at a sprint, he'd invaded her thoughts, her mind and, worse, her heart. Memories of their evening together tumbled through in a kaleidoscope of emotions; her body and mind recalled things she'd forgotten: the way he whispered against her skin so she could feel him smile. The way he'd looked at her, his eyes blazing and intent, as he touched her. The way she'd given herself so completely. She'd felt so wonderfully comfortable, secure and safe with this man.

Or so she'd thought.

In truth, she hadn't been safe at all. She'd been shattered emotionally by the experience, hurt deep inside, her heart bruised. And they hadn't even slept together! Perhaps that was what hurt most of all—what she'd been so ready and eager to give, he hadn't even wanted.

Why? Why had he walked away before they'd even consummated their so-called relationship? She'd been easy pickings, something he hadn't even wanted in the end. And Abby was too proud to ask him why not.

Even though she was glad she'd retired from music, even though she didn't, couldn't, regret her time with Luc, just as she'd said to him, she knew she should. She should certainly be desperate not to repeat the experience.

So why had she spent last night lying sleepless, restless in bed? Reliving, savouring, every memory of that abbreviated evening? Why had her body ached to experience it again?

'It's beef stew and fresh bread tonight for Corner Cottage,' Grace announced cheerfully, pulling the tray of cinnamon buns out of the oven. 'And he wants breakfast as well.'

'Breakfast?' Abby repeated blankly. Just that one innocuous word caused sensation to spin and swirl through her: the thought of lying in bed, tangled among the sheets, sharing bits of sticky bun and sipping coffee. *Breakfast*. A meal she'd never shared with Luc.

And never would.

'Corner Cottage wants more meals?' she asked sharply, and Grace gave her a funny look, her brows drawn together.

'Of course he does. He ordered meals for the entire week, to be delivered every day.'

'Right.' A week of delivering meals to Luc. A week of seeing him again. Abby closed her eyes, unable to face the thought. If she saw him all week, she'd give in. She'd do whatever he wanted. She'd *ask* him…

'Abby, are you all right?'

Abby snapped opened her eyes and forced herself to smile. 'Yes, I'm all right.' She felt as if she were speaking to the absent Luc as much as to Grace. 'I'm perfectly fine,' she said a bit too firmly. Grace raised her brows.

'Am I missing something?'

'No.' Abby wasn't ready to tell Grace how she knew Luc, or even that she knew Luc at all. She'd left that life, all of it, behind her: the piano playing, the fame, that one night. Everything. 'I'm just tired. I'm sorry if I'm not making sense.'

'Do you not want to go to Corner Cottage?' Grace asked, and Abby found herself flushing, wishing she weren't so utterly transparent.

'No, of course not. I mean, of course I do—want to go.' Abby realized she was rambling and closed her mouth, turning to a stack of empty boxes by the door. 'Why wouldn't I?' She reached for an empty box and began to pack it, continuing before Grace could answer that telling question. 'I told you, I'm just tired. I'll head there right away.'

'There are a couple of other deliveries,' Grace said, a shrewd note entering her voice, making Abby wonder if the older woman still saw through her. Probably. 'Cadgwith and Mullion.' She paused. 'You can do those first.'

It took Abby most of the day to make her deliveries, leaving Corner Cottage to last. It was only as she pulled the old van up to the cottage on Carack's high street that she realized she should have gone there first, got it over with, and then she could have used the excuse of having other deliveries to make a quick departure.

Or did she not want a reason to leave, but rather one to stay? Wincing at the revealing nature of that question, Abby slipped out of the van and grabbed the box of meals from the back.

She walked around to the back garden, balancing the heavy box on one hip as she reached for the kitchen door's tarnished brass-knocker, her heart already beginning a slow, relentless drumming. She let the knocker fall once, twice, before waiting. Her skin was clammy, her heart beating so loud and fast now she could feel it reverberating through her entire body.

No one answered the knock. No one came. And, Abby realized with a flash of irritated self-awareness, she was disappointed. She set the box on the ground and reached for her own key; Grace always had spare sets to all the cottages she served.

Abby turned the lock, hoisted the box once more and stepped inside. She couldn't stop herself from looking around, noticing the little things: the single cup and plate left to dry on the drainer by the sink, the heavy woollen socks and muddy hiking-boots drying by the fire, which had dwindled to a few embers in the grate. She peeked in the fridge; besides the leftover lasagne and salad, there was a packet of coffee and a pint of milk.

Quickly she unloaded the meals, her gaze still sliding around the cottage, noticing other things, things telling her about the man she'd never had the chance to know as well as she'd wanted to. A paperback book and a pair of horn-rimmed spectacles lay on the side table by the sofa. He wore glasses? she thought, almost incredulously. Just another thing she hadn't known.

She knew, absolutely knew, she shouldn't go upstairs. She'd delivered the meals, for heaven's sake, there was no reason to go upstairs. No reason at all.

Yet still she found herself tiptoeing up the narrow, twisting steps, her breath caught in her chest. She was spying. Snooping; there could be no other word for it. She should turn back, scuttle out of the back door and drive back to Grace's cottage, relieved she'd managed to avoid Luc today.

She kept climbing.

A peek in the bathroom showed a slightly damp towel neatly folded on the side of the bath, a straight-edge razor and an old-fashioned cake of shaving soap by the sink. She picked up the soap and sniffed it, memory flooding through her at its recognizable woodsy tang. She dropped it as if burned, and wiped her hand on her jeans.

'I've got to get out of here,' she whispered almost frantically, and then turned to peek in the bedroom.

Considering how neat the other rooms were, Abby thought, the bed should have been made, the cream-coloured duvet pulled tight. It wasn't. The bed was deliciously, luxuriously rumpled, and as Abby crept closer she saw the imprint of Luc's head on the pillow. She couldn't keep herself from coming even closer, bending over and breathing in the scent of him on the sheets.

'Abby?'

Abby jumped nearly a foot in the air. She whirled around, her hand clutched to her chest. 'Oh! You—you scared me!'

'Is everything all right?' Luc stood in the doorway, one eyebrow arched, and colour flooded Abby's face. Had what she'd been doing been so appallingly obvious? She'd been smelling his sheets, for heaven's sake. She closed her eyes for a second's respite from the sheer awfulness of the situation, then opened them and forced herself to smile breezily.

'Everything's fine. I was just—checking on things. All part of the service.'

'That's really very…thorough of you,' Luc remarked, and Abby had a terrible feeling she hadn't fooled him at all.

'Yes, well. It's important to be thorough,' she finished lamely. 'So, since everything looks ship-shape, I'll just be going.' She started to inch towards the doorway, conscious that Luc was filling that space. He didn't move.

Abby stood in front of him, her throat and mouth dry, her heart thundering right out of her chest. She swallowed, tried smiling again. 'Luc…?'

He looked down at her, his eyes darkening to the colour of the sea, his mouth tightening. 'I need to give you something.'

'No, you don't,' Abby said quickly. She didn't even know what Luc was talking about, but she knew she had to get out of here before she did something even more stupid—like touching him. Like asking him to touch her. Already her hand lifted of its own accord, trembling with the need to lay it on his chest and feel the hard muscle underneath.

He still stood in the doorway, and to get past him she would have to touch him, brush against him; the thought made her frantic with both longing and despair. 'Please, Luc,' she whispered, hating how broken her voice sounded. 'Please move.'

He hesitated, and Abby saw his own hand was raised. Did he want to touch her? Was he going to? She waited, wanting him to move, wanting him to touch her. Finally, after an endless moment, he dropped his hand and moved out of the way. She scurried past him down the stairs.

Luc followed quickly on her heels. Abby's hand was on the latch of the kitchen door when he spoke.

'Don't go.'

'I have other things to do,' she began desperately, and from behind her shoulder she saw him take something from his pocket.

'I told you, I have something for you.'

Slowly, reluctantly, she turned around. 'All right. What is it?' Luc handed her a slip of paper, and Abby had no idea what it could be until she looked down and blinked. Twice. She held a cheque for a million pounds. She swallowed, feeling sick, and shook her head. 'What is this?'

'I want to see you provided for.'

'A million pounds?' She looked up, blinking back the sting of sudden tears. 'Is that how much it costs to clear your conscience?'

A muscle beat in Luc's neck, his eyes narrowing. 'Consider it a gift.'

Slowly, her fingers trembling, Abby tore the cheque in two. Then she tore it again, and again, until there were a dozen bits of paper fluttering to the floor. 'I don't want your money, Luc,' she said quietly. Her throat ached. 'I wanted *you*. You clearly didn't want me, and a million pounds isn't going to make much difference.'

Luc was silent for a long moment, his eyes dark and hard on hers, the skin around his mouth pale and taut. 'Six months ago I was in a difficult place,' he finally said, his eyes never leaving hers, even though Abby felt as if he'd carved a distance between them, a yawning chasm of misunderstanding and unspoken words and feelings. He drew in a tight, short breath. 'I was married.'

Abby felt her mouth fall open, shock drenching her in a sickening, icy wave. *'Married?'*

Luc swore softly. 'Not *then*. My wife—Suzanne—died six months before we met.' He spoke almost impassively, but Abby saw and sensed an ocean of pain swamping him, rising in his eyes. He averted his head, tension emanating from every line of his body, from the taut curve of his jaw to his hunched shoulder.

'I'm sorry,' she said, and knew it was inadequate. Her mind was spinning, already processing the ramifications of Luc's revelation. Was that why he had left? she wondered dully. Because he'd been *grieving*? She swallowed past the lump in her throat to say, 'You must have loved her very much.'

Luc didn't respond, and Abby wondered if he'd heard her. Clearly he expected this to explain everything, and Abby supposed it did. She couldn't have acted as a replacement for a beloved wife; she'd merely been a brief way to assuage his grief, and in the end she supposed that was why he'd left before they'd made love—he hadn't been able to betray his wife, even in death.

'I left because I knew I couldn't—can't—offer you what you deserve. Need.' He swallowed, the movement jerky, convulsive. 'I don't have that to give, Abby.'

Her throat was tight, her eyes stinging. She nodded once.

Luc stared at the ripped bits of the cheque littering the floor. 'Why don't you take it, Abby?' he said quietly. 'Does it even matter why I'm giving it to you? You need it.'

'Actually, I don't. And it does matter, Luc. Money makes what happened between us sordid. Dirty.' She closed her eyes, forcing herself to continue. 'I thought—' She took a breath; it hurt her lungs. 'I thought we had something that night. I thought it was a *beginning*—but it was just a way for you to lose yourself for a few hours, wasn't it? Even if we had made love, you would have walked away in the morning.' Luc didn't answer, and Abby knew she was right. It shouldn't surprise her, she thought. It shouldn't hurt. Yet it did. She shook her head slowly, turning back to the door. 'Goodbye.' The single word was dragged from her and her fingers curled around the cool metal of the door-latch.

'It wasn't like that.' Luc's voice stilled her, so sad and quiet. 'At least,' he amended, 'I didn't want it to be like that.' Abby waited, unable to move, even though she knew she should. Luc took a step towards her and she slowly turned around. 'That night was one of the best experiences of my life, Abby. I know that sounds trite—a bad line from a pop song, I suppose. But it…' His eyes met and melted into hers. 'It gave me hope at a time when I was utterly in despair.' If the words sounded melodramatic, the tone was not. He sounded matter-of-fact, a little bleak and utterly sincere. Abby forced herself to look away.

'Then why did you leave?' she asked in a voice that was far too lost and little. 'Did you change your mind?' She swallowed, needing to ask the one question her pride had forbidden her to voice. 'Did you not want me any more?'

'Oh, Abby.' Luc's voice was choked, and he took another step towards her so they were only a handspan apart. 'Did I not want you?' he murmured softly in disbelief. He reached out to curl his hands around her shoulders, sliding them up to cup her face, his fingers threading through her hair. It wasn't until he touched her that Abby realized how starved she'd been for the contact, and she closed her eyes, savouring the touch of his fingers against her skin.

'I want you more than I've ever wanted anyone,' he whispered, pressing a kiss against her brow before trailing more kisses along her jawline. Abby shuddered. 'I walked away because I didn't want to hurt you more than I already had.' His lips hovered over hers. 'But I keep coming back, don't I,' he said brokenly, choking on the words. 'I can't leave you alone, even though I know it's the right thing to do.'

'Then don't,' Abby murmured, the words a plea. Right now she didn't care about why he might go or stay. She just wanted this moment to last, to keep him with her—even if it hurt in the end—whether it was for an hour, a night or for ever. 'Don't let me go,' she whispered, and closed the space between them, her lips on his, a moan of deep satisfaction starting low in her throat. How she'd wanted this. Needed it.

The little cottage-bedroom was a world away from the sumptuous suite at Hotel Le Bristol, yet it hardly mattered. Once again the world fell away so all Abby was conscious and achingly aware of was Luc.

Luc, standing before her, his face so serious yet with the faint flicker of a smile on his lips as he surveyed her. Luc, reaching out to slip off her tee-shirt and unbutton her jeans. Abby shrugged out of them easily, standing before him naked, unafraid, unselfconscious.

It was so wonderfully the same as before, and yet, Abby knew, it was also different. *She* was different. Stronger, perhaps. More certain. Yet even as these thoughts occurred to her they melted away when Luc looked at her, touched her; his fingers barely skimmed her skin, and yet still she shuddered.

He smiled. 'I've dreamed of this.'

'So have I,' she confessed in a whisper, and reached for the buttons of his shirt.

In but a few moments they were both naked, and Luc claimed her in a kiss as they somehow, half-stumbling, made it to the bed. From the open window Abby could hear the shushing of sea against sand, the distant cry of a gull. Then she lost the ability to hear, see or even think as Luc went to work with his mouth and his hands. He touched her, treasured her with his body as she writhed in response, until all was lost except for the exquisite sensation rolling through her, consuming her in wave after wave of endless pleasure.

And when the time came for their bodies to join, Abby didn't tense, even though she knew there would be some kind of pain. Whatever discomfort she felt melted quickly away in the growing realization that *this* was what everyone talked about, knew about. This was what she'd been missing. She felt as if she'd been seeing the world through a misty veil without realizing it, and only now could she see and feel clearly. The final piece of her soul, her very self, had slid into place, and she hadn't even known it was missing until now.

Afterwards she lay in the cradle of his arms, the sun slanting golden onto the floorboards. She thought of how she'd imagined this scenario only yesterday morning. Yet how could she have imagined it? The feeling of being in Luc's arms once again—completely, now—was beyond imagining.

She turned to look at him, let her fingers trace the faint stubble on his jaw. His eyes were closed yet she knew he was not asleep. Perhaps he wanted to be, she thought with a tinge of sorrow. Perhaps he was pretending to avoid any awkward conversation, the kind of conversation he hadn't allowed them to have before.

And what could they say now? What was there to say? Luc had made it plain that he had no more to give. No more than this—a second night of pleasure, the completion of what had been promised so long ago.

Was it worth it? The question echoed through her, and Abby closed her eyes, her body still vibrating with the memory of his touch, humming with satiated awareness.

Yes. It had been worth it—even if it still left her sad and always, always wanting more.

Somehow she must have drifted off to asleep, for when she awoke the room was cold and dark, and so was the bed. Luc had gone.

This was his cottage, Abby thought, rolling up to a sitting position. She slipped into her tee-shirt, leaving her legs bare as she crept from the bedroom. Surely he hadn't hightailed it out of his own cottage? Yet hadn't he done it before? The hotel room had been his as well. Had he actually left her a second time?

She walked slowly down the stairs, peeking around the corner. Luc sat in the little parlour, a tumbler of whisky cradled in his hands, his expression distant and bleak.

She stood there, feeling faintly ridiculous in just her shirt, and she shivered as a gust of cool air caught her.

Luc turned his head and his gaze held hers; there was an ocean of unspoken words between them. When he finally spoke his words were both a command and a plea: 'Come here.'

And, just like that, she came. She didn't even think about it, didn't even consider saying no. She just went and stood before him uncertainly before Luc reached up and pulled her easily onto his lap. She curled into him all too naturally, tucking her legs under her, pressing her cheek against his chest. Luc stroked her hair, the movement gentle, repetitive, almost lulling her to sleep. Neither of them spoke.

The silence lengthened, growing more poignant and even sorrowful in the lack of words, the lack of anything they could say. Abby's heart ached with the effort of steeling herself for Luc's explanations, apologies: *I'm sorry. This is all I have.*

Yet he didn't say anything, and somehow that made it both better and worse. It made Abby wonder if he knew what she was thinking, if he knew all the things she didn't want to hear.

After another long moment Luc finally stirred, his arms still around Abby. Wordlessly he scooped her up. Abby's arms came around him as a matter of instinct, and, still without speaking, he carried her back upstairs.

He laid her on the bed, his eyes meeting hers, pleading for understanding—forgiveness. And Abby gave it, reaching up to twine her arms around his neck, pulling him down to her in an endless kiss that was apology, atonement and supplication.

If this is all Luc could give, then she would take it. Eagerly. She would make this moment—this night—last for ever; she would sear it into her memory, write it on her heart. As Luc lay on the bed with her, deepening the kiss with aching hunger, Abby knew it was also a farewell.

When she woke again Luc was sleeping next to her in the bed, one arm over his head, his face relaxed in sleep. Abby propped herself on one elbow and watched him for a moment, savouring the look of peace and happiness on his face, the slight smile of sleep, of dreams. Perhaps of memory. She let her fingertip run the length of his cheek, then his jaw, and then the curve of his eyebrow, as if by these simple touches she would remember the feel of him. He stirred slightly at the caress, and reluctantly she let her hand fall away.

Then, before her courage could fail her, she slipped from the bed and quickly put on her clothes. Luc stirred again, and before he woke Abby went hurriedly from the room. She didn't look back.

CHAPTER EIGHT

IT TOOK Abby six weeks. Six weeks of regretting her decision to slip away from Luc as he slept; six weeks of knowing that had been her only choice, even as her heart cried out otherwise. Six weeks of waiting for Luc to find her, call her, write to her—something—even though she knew in her heart he wouldn't. He never did. The silence was complete and unending.

Six weeks, she thought starkly, of being utterly miserable. And six weeks to realize their night together had resulted in more than her broken heart.

'Have you been cooking with onions?' she asked Grace one afternoon. The weather was drizzly and grey and matched her mood.

Grace looked up from the quiche she was taking out of the oven. 'I sliced an onion four hours ago,' she said, eyebrows raised. 'Is that what you are referring to?'

Abby made a face. 'I suppose; the smell has put me off lately, for some reason.'

Grace chuckled. 'If I didn't know you better, I'd say you were pregnant.' Abby froze, and the laughter died on Grace's lips. 'Abby...'

'Right.' Abby tried to smile, laugh. Both efforts were miserable failures, making her sound like some horrible, mechanical pull-toy. Grace wasn't fooled for a minute.

'Abby,' she said, and then crossed the room in a few quick steps to pull her into a hug. 'I'm sorry, that was callous of me. I just didn't think you were seeing anyone.'

'I'm not,' Abby replied bleakly, and Grace's arms tightened around her.

'And that was callous as well. Good Lord, I'm not used to this.' She stepped back, surveying Abby's pale, drained face with maternal anxiety. 'What are you going to do? There's obviously a chance.'

'I suppose there is,' Abby agreed numbly. Luc had used a condom, but accidents happened. Mistakes happened. Her hands crept instinctively to her middle, as if the tiny life—if there even was one—might hear those horrible words: mistake; accident.

No.

'We'll buy a pregnancy test. They're so quick these days, and reliable too.'

'Yes, they are, aren't they?' What an inane conversation, Abby thought, her mind still numb, frozen. They both sounded like they were starring in an advert for modern pregnancy tests. What did it matter how quick or reliable a pregnancy test was? Her mind and body were already screaming the truth: the nausea, the fatigue, the tightness of her jeans' waistband. She hadn't put it all together because it had never occurred to her, not even for one moment, that she might actually be pregnant. Yet, now that the possibility had been presented to her, it was all too glaringly obvious. Anyone with a rudimentary knowledge of biology, or who'd been in a high-school health class, could have confirmed her symptoms and offered the correct diagnosis.

Pregnant. With Luc's child.

She looked up at Grace, who was gazing at her in obvious concern, and summoned a smile. 'Yes. Right. Well, I think I'll go the chemist's, then.'

'Do you want me to come?'

'No. No, thank you. I'll do it alone.'

And so she did, driving to the chemist's in Helston, the ten-minute trip a blur. Her mind felt permanently stuck in one gear, one loop—pregnant. Pregnant. Pregnant.

The clerk at the till was a pimply teenaged boy, but he didn't even bat an eyelid as Abby pushed the pregnancy test with its glaring pink writing across to him.

'That'll be ten pounds,' he told her in a bored voice.

Inanely Abby found herself saying, 'That's quite expensive, isn't it?'

He stared at her. 'That's ten quid.'

'Right.' She handed him the note.

She ducked into a local café's toilet to take the test. Somehow she couldn't bear the thought of bringing it back to Grace's and having her hover while Abby did what was necessary.

It only took a few minutes. A few minutes, and then a lifetime of accepting the reality. Two lines on the little plastic stick; she really was pregnant.

Abby let herself out of the bathroom and drove back to Grace's, the trip just as much a blur as it had been before. As soon as Grace saw her face—Abby couldn't fathom what her own expression was, for she didn't even know how she was feeling—she wrapped her in a hug.

'Oh, love.' They were both silent, and then Grace pulled away. 'You know I'll support you one-hundred percent, no matter what you do?'

Abby nodded, although even now she knew she had no choice, not really. Already that little life inside her had taken root, begun to grow. He—or she—was part of her, part of Luc. She would keep the child. She would have Luc's baby.

Lingering over breakfast in his hotel suite in Paris, Luc turned to the arts pages of the newspaper without thinking. It was what he always did, scanning the headlines and bylines with a distracted air, unable to voice even to himself what, or who, he was looking for.

Then he saw it.

Piano Prodigy—pregnant?

The photo was a blurry shot of Abby walking down a street in London. The newspaper had helpfully added a red circle to highlight the slight swell of her middle.

Even as realization slammed into him, Luc found himself thinking, *why is Abby in London*? What had happened? What was she doing?

He read the article in a matter of seconds; it was spurious speculation about the 'Piano Prodigy's sudden retirement', her disappointing reviews last year and then her mysterious reappearance in London this week.

It only took up a few inches of space on the third page of the arts section. Abby, Luc realized, was hardly news any more.

Yet she was, it seemed, pregnant. And he knew without even a flicker of doubt that, if there was indeed a baby, then it was his.

He pushed the paper away, unfocused, unseeing, his mind spinning with thoughts he could barely articulate. The coffee at his elbow grew cold and the sun rose in the sky, casting longer and longer shadows on the floor.

Finally, as if shaking himself from a dream, Luc rose. He reached for his mobile phone, flicking it open and punching buttons. When his assistant answered, he spoke tersely. 'I need the jet. This morning.'

'It's in Avignon, and it's already noon.'

Impatience bit at him. 'Have it brought to Paris by four o'clock. I want to be in Cornwall by six.'

'Oui, Monsieur le Comte.'

Luc snapped his phone shut and gazed out at the River

Seine winding through the city. The cherry trees were just beginning to blossom. Then, turning away from the charming
sight, he prepared to pack for his trip to England…to find
Abby.

Cornwall was in the throes of early spring. The hedgerows
were budding with sorrel and bluebells as Luc made his way
along the narrow coast-road into Carack. He'd rented a one-
bedroom flat in a large Edwardian villa; Corner Cottage was
already let. Perhaps that was better, Luc thought starkly, for
surely the past could not be retrieved or recaptured?

What they'd had *was* past, gone. He'd felt the truth of it
echo in his empty heart when Abby had left their bed six
months ago. Her departure had been an eloquent, silent
farewell—a choice, Luc knew, that had been best for both of
them. It had to be.

Except, if she truly was pregnant with his child, then that
changed everything. How, Luc could not quite yet envision
or articulate. He couldn't marry, couldn't give, couldn't love.
Yet he also knew his responsibility was to his child, and he
would not shirk it. Not this time. His fingers tightened around
the steering wheel. He needed to find the truth. He needed
to find Abby.

Dusk was falling soft and violet over the sea as Abby let
herself into the cottage where she rented a bedroom. Although
basic accommodation, it was cozy and picturesque. After
years of living in hotels, Abby found she preferred this comfortable room in a tiny thatched-cottage, with its fluffy
double-bed covered with a patchwork quilt, an old dresser and
a washstand in the corner.

Upstairs in her bedroom, she let out a long, weary sigh and
her hands went instinctively to her lower back, to rub the in-
sistent dull ache that had lodged there since she'd first learned

she was pregnant over three months ago—three long, bewildering, uncertain months.

'Hello, Abby.'

Abby let out a gasp of surprise and whirled around, her hands dropping to her sides.

Luc sat in the battered chair in the corner, one leg neatly crossed over the other, his fingers steepled under his chin. In the twilit gloom, Abby couldn't read the expression on his face, but she knew it wasn't anything good. His voice too was terribly neutral.

'Luc!' She struggled to find something to say, to make sense of the emotions coursing through her in a tangle of feeling. Then she narrowed her eyes. 'How did you get in?'

'The locals are very friendly, especially when I told them I was surprising you…being the father of your child, you see.'

Abby groaned aloud and reached for her bedside tablelamp, switching it on, grateful for its comforting, normal glow. Her mind was spinning, and she was torn between fury, fear and a completely unreasonable joy at seeing him again. 'I'm sure you quite intimidated them.'

'Perhaps,' Luc replied with a negligent shrug. 'I see you didn't correct my assumption—I am the father of this child?' He gestured towards her middle; the fabric of her tee-shirt was taut over her growing bump.

Abby let out a short laugh. 'You mean, rather than the *other* lover I had while you were here?'

'Don't be sarcastic, Abby.'

'Don't tell me what to be,' Abby flashed. 'You don't have the right.'

'Oh?' Luc's voice was soft and dangerous, his eyes narrowed to blazing-blue slits. 'And let me ask you about *your* rights—is it your right not to tell me about my own child?'

Abby laughed again, shaking her head. 'You really have

some nerve, Luc. I don't even know your last name, or where you live, besides "the Languedoc"…if you really do live there. I don't know anything about you. So how,' she finished, her voice rising in fury, 'was I supposed to tell you about your child?'

Luc didn't even blink. 'I gave my name to your employer when I ordered the meals for Corner Cottage. You could have asked her.'

'I could have,' Abby allowed with a shrug, infuriated all the more by his refusal to apologize or explain. 'And maybe I should have. But frankly you've been giving me the rather strong impression of not wanting to be found, and I don't think I should have to be Sherlock Holmes to find you.'

Luc rose from the chair in one swift, graceful movement, crossing the small space to stand in front of Abby before she had time to react. He lowered his face close to hers, his eyes glittering, his voice low. 'I think Sherlock Holmes is a bit of an exaggeration. And who,' he asked softly, 'really was the one who didn't want to be found? Who left in the middle of the night this time, Abby?'

She raised her chin, refusing to move, to back down. 'Doesn't feel good, does it?'

'So that's what it was—some kind of revenge?'

She sighed and shook her head, suddenly weary. Her back still ached, and she desperately wanted some paracetemol. 'No, not really,' she said after a moment. 'I don't know what it was.' She turned away from him, searching through the medicine cabinet above the sink for the much-needed tablets. 'I just didn't want to be there in the morning for some wretched conversation about how you couldn't give me what I needed, blah, blah, blah,' she finally said, and laughed, the sound sad and slightly bitter. 'And I'd have had to nod and smile and say I completely understood because, after all, I knew what I was getting into, right?'

'Right,' Luc said after a moment, his voice quiet and thoughtful, and even a little sad. It seemed as if all the self-righteous fury had drained out of them both. 'Is that what you think would have happened?'

She turned to him, tablets in hand, one eyebrow arched in disbelief. 'Are you saying differently?'

Slowly Luc shook his head. 'What matters now is the fact that you are carrying my child. That changes everything.'

Abby felt something settle coldly inside her bones at the grim finality of his words. 'I don't see how it changes much of anything,' she finally said, turning back to the sink to fill a glass with tap water. She took a sip and swallowed two pills, closing her eyes as fatigue threatened to overwhelm her, not for the first time that day. She'd had no idea that pregnancy would be so exhausting.

'Why were you in London?' Luc asked abruptly. 'You weren't seeking…some procedure?'

'You mean an abortion?' Abby gestured to her burgeoning belly. 'Obviously not.'

'That would be a terrible thing to do, to abort my child without telling me,' he said quietly.

'About as terrible as leaving me stark naked in your hotel room to be woken up by the maid?' Abby quipped, and then added in a false French accent, 'The gentleman checked out late last night…'

Luc had the grace to wince. 'I'm sorry it happened that way,' he said. 'But we've gone over this already, Abby, and I've apologized before. Are we going to keep having this conversation?'

Abby sighed. 'No, we're not. We don't need to have any conversation.' She turned away, but Luc reached out to touch her shoulder. It was a light touch, yet it stilled her.

'Why are you so angry with me, Abby? You are angrier now than ever before. Is it the child—?'

'No, it is not *the child*,' Abby snapped. 'It's…' She blew out her breath, too weary even to articulate the emotions coursing through her. She didn't really understand them herself. 'I don't know what it is, Luc. Pregnancy hormones? All I can say is I'm starting to dislike how you breeze in and out of my life as it suits you, and I never know if you're coming or going, or when, or…anything.'

'I was not the one who left last time,' Luc reminded her.

'It was only a matter of time, wasn't it?'

He shook his head. 'I don't—' He stopped, and Abby saw the regret darken his eyes, stiffen his shoulders. Maybe he wanted to feel more, she thought sadly, give more, but he just couldn't.

'It doesn't matter,' she said quietly. 'What's past is past.'

'Yes, and it is the future we must be thinking of.' He gestured to her bump once more.

Abby felt a chill of foreboding. Of course, it was obvious. Luc had come back because he'd somehow discovered she was pregnant, which could only mean one thing—he felt some sort of responsibility for her baby. His baby. Of course he would, she thought wearily. Luc had the biggest guilt complex of any man she'd ever met. Of course he would take on the responsibility of his own child.

But what did that mean practically, realistically, day to day?

Did he want to be in his child's life? In hers?

It was too much to take in, to accept, and Abby fought against a sudden double wave of nausea and dizziness. She closed her eyes and swayed, only for a second, but Luc noticed.

'*Mon Dieu,*' he said, sounding both angry and afraid. 'You look like you're going to faint.'

'No,' Abby denied, her eyes still closed as she groped for a chair. 'I'm just tired, and I need to sit down. I haven't eaten—'

'You are—what?—four, five months' pregnant and you haven't eaten?'

She sank into a chair and opened her eyes to look wryly at Luc. 'Five. And I was going to say, before you interrupted me, that I haven't eaten *in several hours*. I need to snack compulsively.' She leaned her head against the back of the chair and closed her eyes once more. 'There are some peanut-butter crackers in my bag, if you wouldn't mind getting them for me.'

Luc rifled through her handbag. Idly Abby wondered what revealing items might be in there—an old lipstick, a half-eaten scone?—before weariness claimed her once more.

'Here.' Luc handed her the packet of crackers, and Abby nibbled on one gratefully.

'Thank you.'

'Have you had dinner? If the village has a pub or restaurant…'

'We'll have everyone talking then,' Abby said, and tried to laugh. She couldn't quite pull it off.

'I don't care what a bunch of fishermen and holidaymakers have to say,' Luc replied brusquely. 'Or what anyone has to say, for that matter. You need to eat.'

Abby smiled ruefully. 'You've really gone all cave man on me, haven't you? The need to protect, and all that.'

'It's common sense,' Luc replied, his voice still sounding terse, and Abby couldn't argue with that.

'All right,' she said, and rose from the chair. 'But, since it's your idea, you can pay.'

Luc made a sound halfway between a grunt and a snort, and Abby took it to mean that of course there had never been any other option—for eating or paying.

She reached for her bag, and Luc opened the door of her bedroom. The cottage was dark, and Abby fumbled for the light switch on the stairs.

'Does no one else live here?' Luc asked, and she shook her head.

'It's a holiday cottage. The owners come on the weekend sometimes, and in the summer, but they like me to keep an eye on it in return for a lower rent and use of the kitchen.'

'So you're alone?' Luc demanded and Abby nearly groaned.

'Yes, but, as a fully functioning adult, I think I can manage.'

Luc made no reply, and Abby braced herself for more such questions. Clearly Luc was going to find fault with every aspect of her life now that she was pregnant with his baby.

They walked down the village high-street next to the sea, the fishing boats were half pulled-up onto the muddy shore. The water lapped hungrily at their sides, a restless, slapping sound that for some reason put Abby on edge. They didn't speak until they arrived at the village's only pub, a white-washed building with a thatched roof.

Luc opened the door, gesturing for her to enter before him.

'Thank you,' Abby murmured, and entered the dim, cozy interior. Within moments Luc was speaking to the owner, and he quickly arranged for a private room in the back of the pub.

'Did you order as well?' Abby asked as she followed him past the long, mahogany bar with a row of openly curious fishermen nursing their pints.

'The vegetable soup and steak,' Luc replied. 'Obviously you need to keep your strength up.'

Abby shook her head, slipping off her coat as she surveyed the private room with its fireplace and cozy table for two. 'Thanks for that consideration,' she said as she sat down, and Luc cocked his head.

'You've lost your innocence.'

In response, Abby patted her bump. 'That happened a while ago.'

'I don't mean that.' He slid into the seat across from her, steepling his fingers under his chin again. 'When I met you in Paris you were starry-eyed, enchanted by everything. You seem more…cynical now.'

'Just realistic,' Abby quipped, but Luc shook his head.

'Was it because of me? Because of what happened between us?'

'It was a lot of things, Luc,' Abby told him. 'Yes, of course *you*, that night, were part of it. But so was losing all the money I thought I had.' She swallowed and made herself go on. 'Losing the joy of music. Losing everything I'd based my whole self on.' She shook her head, not wanting to drown in the old memories. 'I'm not cynical, you know, or even realistic. I'm just me. I'm not sure I even knew who I was until I stopped playing piano. I finally feel like I have the freedom to be me—to say what I want, do what I want—because there are no expectations. No rules. No public or press to perform for.' She took a sip of water that a waiter had poured before leaving. 'You probably can't imagine how wonderful that feels.'

'Have you played piano again?'

She shook her head. 'No. It's better that way…for now.' Even if sometimes she woke up in the middle of the night to find her arms raised, fingers splayed, playing in her sleep. Even if now her fingers drummed out a rhythm on her thigh and she heard notes in her head. Far worse was the thought, the fear, that she would play and she wouldn't feel anything—no connection to the music, no joy. Nothing…just as Luc felt nothing.

Luc was watching, his head tilted thoughtfully to one side. 'You're happy,' he said, and it was more of a statement than a question.

Abby considered. 'I'm content,' she said finally. 'I'm honest enough to admit I don't want to haul boxes of food around for the rest of my life, even in a place as pretty as Cornwall. But for now—'

Luc held up a hand, his brows drawn together in an incredulous frown. 'You're five months' pregnant and you're still hauling boxes?'

'I asked my midwife, and it's fine as long as I don't strain.'

'Abby, you're doing heavy manual labour! That is *not* fine.' Luc dropped his hand, placing it flat on the table, his eyes narrowing. 'And I won't allow it.'

'Oh?' Abby found herself rising to the challenge, almost enjoying this battle of wills. She'd been bowled over by Luc the first time she'd met him, and still powerless to resist him the second. Now at last, third time lucky, she'd be strong. 'And how do you intend to stop me?'

Luc swore under his breath. 'Shall I drag you by the hair? Lock you in your bedroom? Or can we be reasonable about this?'

Abby found herself smiling properly for the first time in days. Maybe weeks. 'It depends what your definition of reasonable is.'

Luc sat back in his chair, running a hand through his hair. He looked weary then, Abby saw, and, strangely, even a little vulnerable.

'I would like you not to lift heavy things,' he said finally. 'Or live alone. You had one dizzy spell—what if you had another, on the stairs?'

'I won't.'

'You don't know that. And who is there to help? I met your employer when I came here today. She is a nice enough woman, but her back is bad, as you must know. She can do very little.'

'I don't need Grace to do anything,' Abby protested.

Luc shook his head. 'Do you have other friends, people to call?'

Abby flushed. 'Yes, of course I have friends,' she said, but Luc's words hit home. She might have friends, but they were not the sort you called during a crisis, or in the middle of the night. They were the kind you said hello to in the street, or chatted to briefly in the shop, and nothing more.

'Regardless,' Luc continued, determined and implacable, 'we are not addressing the main issue here, which is what we will do after the child is born.'

A waiter came in with their food, giving Abby a moment to collect her scattered thoughts and wits. What did Luc mean, *we*?

But of course, Abby realized, she knew what he meant. This time, he wasn't going away. But only because of the baby.

Not because of her.

Which was, she supposed, at least one reason why she hadn't sought him out after learning she was pregnant—she didn't want to be his charity case.

The waiter left, and Abby toyed with her food, her appetite vanished. She couldn't think of a thing to say. Luc, apparently, did not have that problem.

'There is no question,' he said, taking a sip of wine, 'of me not being in my own child's life.'

Abby still couldn't think of anything to say. She wanted to argue, but how? Why? On a theoretical level, she believed fathers should be involved in their children's lives if they wanted to be. Of course. Yet how was that going to work on a practical basis? How could Luc be involved in her baby's life, in *her* life? How, without her heart breaking, her hopes dying just a little every day?

'Well,' she finally said, trying to sound businesslike. 'Yes, of course. I can see that.' She took a bite of her dinner, although she could barely taste it. 'Perhaps we could arrange visits every other weekend…' She trailed off, for Luc was slowly, resolutely shaking his head.

'I won't be fobbed off with the occasional weekend, Abby.'

A sudden spurt of fury fuelled her briefly. 'If you had nothing to offer me, Luc,' she asked, 'why would you have something for my child?'

'*Our* child,' he corrected, and Abby supposed that said it all.

She closed her eyes, fighting the mental and physical exhaustion once more. 'To tell you the truth,' she finally said, 'I hadn't thought much beyond the baby's birth. I've been terribly ill—not *really* ill,' she amended hurriedly. 'But nauseous. Morning sickness. So I haven't been able to do much more than take each day as it comes.' She let out her breath slowly. 'I suppose that will have to change.'

'Yes.'

She lifted her gaze to meet his. 'But I don't know how yet, and I'm not prepared to decide such things this evening.'

Luc shrugged. 'As you wish. I can be here for a week, and then I must return to France. We have a bit of time.'

'A bit', Abby thought. In other words, not much.

They ate the rest of the meal in virtual silence, and with a pang Abby remembered their first meal together, at Hotel Le Bristol. The hours had flown by, and she'd never felt at a loss for what to say. She'd chatted and laughed and been entirely at ease.

'What is wrong?' Luc asked abruptly, and Abby's gaze flew to his. She realized she'd let out a little sigh of remembrance, even of longing, without noticing.

'I'm just tired,' she said. 'I should go home to bed.'

Luc nodded, and within minutes he'd paid the bill and was ushering her out of the emptying pub, one arm around her shoulders.

He dropped his arm once they were on the street, and Abby shivered from the chilly early March wind blowing off the sea. She felt bereft from the loss of his touch, and from something deeper still. What had happened to the two people who had enjoyed that evening—that night—together? she wondered. Where had they gone?

For surely she was a different person—more grown up, more practical, perhaps even cynical, as Luc had suggested. Yet she was more capable too, more in charge of herself and her own destiny. Except, what was she thinking? Abby's mouth twisted in a truly cynical smile. She wasn't in charge of anything. Luc had just about told her tonight that he would be involved in their child's life, that he didn't want her working for Grace; basically, that he would be the one calling the shots. Forging her destiny.

Abby wasn't sure she had the strength, or even the will, to fight him.

She shoved her hands deeper into the pockets of her parka and bent her head against the wind.

Luc stopped her at the door of the cottage as she fumbled with the key. 'I'll see you in safely, and then I should go.'

Abby's cheeks burned. Had he actually thought she expected him to stay? *Wanted* him to stay?

Yet she could not deny the lurch of longing inside her when she thought of what that would have meant.

'Of course.'

'And we'll talk tomorrow.'

'Fine.' She shoved the key into the lock and tried to turn, but in her anxious state it jammed and she was left pushing with increasing frustration until Luc's hand curled around hers.

'Let me.'

'I'm fine!' she protested, and then watched helplessly as his fingers smoothly, easily, turned the key and the door swung inwards. She turned around to face him. Luc's hand was still on the door, so she was effectively imprisoned in the cage made by his body, his face all too close as he gazed down at her. Desire—unbidden, unwanted—swamped her.

'I don't know if I can do this,' she whispered.

'I'm here to help,' Luc replied, and he reached with one hand to gently touch her cheek. Abby raised her hand to curl her fingers around his. She meant to remove his hand, but somehow she ended up keeping it there, pressed against her cold cheek.

'I'm not talking about the practical side,' she said quietly. 'This, Luc. Us. Or the fact that there is no "us" any more. There never really was. Just two nights, that's all.' She swallowed. 'It's too hard.'

Luc was silent for a long moment, his fingers still touching her cheek. 'I will try to make things as easy and comfortable for you as possible, Abby.' He smiled sadly. 'I'm afraid that's all I can do.'

Abby nodded, her throat suddenly tight. It was her own fault, she supposed, for feeling this way. Feeling too much, when Luc couldn't feel enough. Somehow she would have to get through it, push past the emotion, the hurt and, worst of all, the treacherous hope that just being with him caused inside her, setting her soul to sail.

She thought sadly how once she would have dreamed of a time such as this: she was carrying Luc's child, and he was here with her, ready to love and protect. Love and protect the baby, of course, not her. Never her. Nodding in silent acceptance of Luc's offer, she wondered when and how it had all gone so horribly wrong.

CHAPTER NINE

OF COURSE, it happened on the stairs, just as Luc had said and feared it would. After a long, restless night, Abby skipped breakfast in an attempt to get to Grace's and start her round of deliveries on time. One moment she was hurrying down the stairs, car keys in hand, parka thrown over her arm…the next, she wasn't sure what happened, or how, only that the world seemed to blacken at the corners, like the edges of an old photograph curling upwards. And then she wasn't aware of anything at all.

When she woke, she felt as if she were swimming upwards through water, to a surface in the distance hazy with sunshine. She opened her eyes slowly, blinking several times as the world came into focus once more. She was in a hospital bed, and Luc was sitting next to her.

It took another couple of blinks before she was able to see him properly. He radiated tension. He was leaning forward in the hard, plastic chair that was painted a virulent shade of orange, his forearms braced on his thighs, his face drawn into a rather ferocious expression.

'Oh, come on,' Abby said, and was amazed at how rusty her voice sounded. She tried to smile. 'I can't look that bad, surely?'

At the first syllable she uttered, Luc's gaze jerked to hers, and for one glorious second his whole countenance—every-thing about him—lightened; Abby felt as if she could sing with joy. In that moment, that second, she felt anything was possible. Then he turned grim again, his expression closing up like a fan as he reached out to touch her forehead with his fingertips, checking for fever.

'You've been out cold for over an hour.'

'Really?' The idea that she'd been involuntarily unconscious for such a length of time provoked a mild curiosity, followed by a far deeper foreboding as Luc stared at her incredulously.

'Yes, really. I found you passed out at the bottom of the stairs—you're lucky you didn't break your neck!'

'And that the door was open,' Abby murmured.

'Yes. And, speaking of, why was the door open?' Luc demanded. 'Did you keep it open all night? Anyone could have—'

'There are no more than seventy-five residents in the village, Luc,' Abby said, and then her hand flew to her middle as a new, terrifying thought dawned. 'Am I—is the baby—?'

'The doctor listened to the baby's heartbeat as soon as I brought you in,' Luc told her. He touched her hand briefly in reassurance. 'Everything sounds fine, but she wants to do a scan just in case.'

Abby nodded, her hand still hovering protectively over her bump, relief pouring through her and making her feel weak. The possibility of a threat to her baby made her heart thud with anxiety and fear even though the danger had passed.

A few minutes later the doctor entered her room, a trim woman in her thirties with a neat bun of light-brown hair.

'Had a bit of a scare,' she remarked as she squeezed a cold blob of clear gel onto Abby's bare stomach. 'We ran some blood tests, and it turns out you're a bit anaemic. Have you been taking your pre-natal vitamins?'

'Yes, every day,' Abby replied. She resisted the urge to

shoot Luc a knowing glance. Undoubtedly he thought that she hadn't been taking care of herself properly.

'Well, then,' the doctor said comfortably, 'we'll add an iron supplement to that. Now, let's just take a look, shall we?' She took the electric wand and began to prod Abby's bump rather vigorously. A second later a blurry black-and-white image came onto the screen, and Abby gasped aloud at the sight of the little life moving around, arms and legs, the tiny heart beating fast and furious.

'The little fellow looks all right, then,' the doctor said with a smile.

Abby cried, 'You can tell? It's a boy?'

'That's actually a gender-neutral term for the moment,' she replied with a laugh. 'But I can tell you if you want. First, though, let's check everything else. According to your due date, you were meant to have a scan next week anyway, so we might as well just have done with it a bit early.'

Abby nodded eagerly, and then listened in rapt attention as the doctor went through all the parts of the baby. Healthy parts—heart, liver, lungs. Everything was 'spot on and developing normally'.

'That's wonderful,' Abby whispered, and she glanced at Luc. He was staring at the ultrasound screen as if mesmerized, and perhaps he was. 'I can't believe the baby is moving so much,' Abby said. 'I can't feel a thing.'

'You will soon enough. Now, there is a slight concern here.' The doctor tapped the screen, and Abby's breath hitched. She didn't like the sound of a 'concern', slight or not. Her hand scrabbled on the sheet and then stilled when Luc found it, lacing her fingers with his, his touch steady and warm.

'You have a partial placenta previa,' the doctor said. 'It's a fairly common condition, where the placenta is blocking the opening of your cervix, but it presents some danger to the baby during delivery, so we need to monitor it. With any luck it will resolve itself before your nine months are up, and no worries.'

She smiled kindly at Abby, who could feel her face draining of colour as worry bit at her nerves and thoughts. 'However, you'll need to take it a bit easy until then. No running up and down stairs, no lifting heavy things—and, unfortunately, no sex.' She smiled apologetically at Luc. 'We'll book you for another scan in a month, and it might have cleared up by then. Now.' She brought her hands together in a soft clap, her eyes glinting merrily. 'Do you want to know if you're having a boy or girl?'

Abby glanced at Luc. 'Do you want to know?' she asked, and he paused, hesitating, before uttering with heartfelt sincerity, 'Yes.'

'A girl,' the doctor said. 'A beautiful baby girl.'

A girl. A daughter. Luc could scarcely believe it. His mind spun as he helped Abby up from her bed and then guided her out of the hospital. He had a baby girl.

'You should eat something,' he told Abby. She looked far too pale. The moment when he'd seen her at the bottom of the stairs had been the worst of his life—second-worst, he amended grimly, but utterly terrifying nonetheless. She'd looked so still and waxen, as beautiful, fragile and lifeless as a doll. For a horrifying second he'd thought she was dead, and it had felt like his world had stopped, as if he had stopped.

Then she'd let out a low moan, and he'd sprung into action, pushing away the thoughts, fears and memories as he'd sought to make her safe, to protect her and their child in a way he hadn't been able to protect before.

He had scooped her up, amazed at how light she felt even when pregnant. Her head had fallen back, revealing the long, vulnerable column of her throat. Luc had choked on a sob of desperation.

No. Not again. Not this time...

Still the feelings had come, the helplessness, the hopelessness, the bleak despair. And then the regret, the guilt. He should have insisted she stay with him. He should have been with her. He should have...he should have... So many shoulds.

It hurt to feel this much, to fear this much. The hour in the hospital room, watching Abby breathe in and out without so much as fluttering an eyelash, had been an utter agony, a torment of uncertainty.

What if? What if? What if?

Then, when she'd opened her eyes, he'd felt as if life had been given back to him, precious, fleeting. And the giddy rush of hope had hurt too, because he knew it couldn't last. He'd clamped down on it, pushed the emotions away and accepted the mantle of cold numbness that had, with time, become his only armour against the pain of feeling.

'We can stop at the chemists' to get the prescription for iron tablets,' he told Abby now as he helped her into the car, keeping his voice brisk. 'And then we should have some lunch.'

'I need to see Grace,' Abby murmured. She still looked pale and dazed, and Luc wondered what she was thinking, feeling. His hands tightened on the steering wheel.

'You'll have to give her your notice.'

Abby leaned her head back against the seat and closed her eyes. 'I suppose.'

'There's no *supposing* about it.'

'Oh, Luc.' She shook her head wearily. 'Give it a rest.'

Impatience—and, worse, fear—gnawed at him, as persistent and ferocious as a rat. He couldn't let go of it, couldn't stop wanting to manage. To control. To keep Abby safe, as he never had Suzanne.

He needed to stop, he told himself. He needed to relax. Abby was a competent adult, fully capable of making her own decisions and taking charge of her own life; she'd shown him that. Yet he couldn't quite stop himself from saying, 'Fine. But we need to make some decisions soon.'

'Fine,' she murmured, sounding almost asleep, and Luc finally forced himself to leave it at that.

She was so tired. The buzz of seeing her baby on the scan had evaporated for the moment in the cold reality of what this meant. She couldn't take care of herself after all. She needed Luc. She didn't want to need him, to be dependent on him. To be his burden.

Abby couldn't process it any more, couldn't consider all the implications. She certainly couldn't have the necessary conversation with Luc. Not yet, anyway, while her head still ached and her vision swam. She closed her eyes once more.

They arrived back at the cottage, and Luc helped Abby out of the car. He didn't speak, and Abby was grateful for the silence. She let him help her up the stairs—she didn't have much choice, really—and settle her in bed. She remained as docile as a child.

Luc left, murmuring that he'd be back soon. Abby must have slept, for when she woke the sun was already starting to descend in a darkening sky and the room was dim.

'Luc?' she called out, blinking sleep from her eyes, her voice rusty again.

'I'm here.' He switched on a lamp, and Abby found herself smiling at him, a ridiculously wide grin; she was too happy to see him. He was *here*. 'I brought you some soup, if you can manage it. I think that knock on the head was a bit harder than anyone thought, although the doctors did rule out the possibility of concussion.'

'Perhaps it was,' Abby agreed. 'And, actually, I'm starving.'

'That's a good sign. Just a moment.' He left the room, returning a few minutes later with a tray of food. Abby looked down at the steaming bowl of soup, chunk of fresh bread, and cup of tea—milky and sweet, just as she liked it. She felt tears rise behind her lids and lodge in her throat in an aching lump. She couldn't bear him to be so kind, so utterly thoughtful, and yet know that he was only doing it because of the baby. She wanted it to be because of her.

She wanted him to love her.

Abby pushed these thoughts away, managing a smile as she took a sip of soup. 'Thank you. It's delicious.'

'Courtesy of the pub,' Luc told her. 'Cooking, alas, is not one of my talents.'

'Mine neither.'

'Yes, I remember—learning to cook was right under flying a kite in a list of things you wanted to do.'

'And still haven't learned,' Abby replied with a shrug and a smile, although she was more touched than she could admit by Luc's memory. Luc was staring at her in a thoughtful, assessing way that she didn't quite like. She turned back to her soup.

'Abby,' Luc finally said, his voice turning gentle, 'we need to discuss the future.' Abby said nothing. The lump in her throat had grown bigger, and her eyes burned. She stared down at her soup, blinking hard. 'You cannot continue here as you are,' Luc said, his voice low and steady. 'Surely you see that?'

'I understand,' Abby said after a long moment, 'that I can't continue lifting boxes.'

'Or living alone, or working as you have been. None of it—you heard the doctor.'

'What am I supposed to do, then?' Abby demanded. 'Lie in bed for the next four months?'

'No, of course not,' Luc replied after a brief pause, making Abby think that was exactly what he would like her to do. She was carrying precious cargo, after all. 'But you need to rest and relax, without worry for money or meals or any of that.'

'That does sound nice,' Abby said with a little laugh. 'Although—'

'I want you to come to France.' Luc cut her off abruptly. 'With me.'

Abby stilled, his words reverberating through her. Then she looked up, and was caught by the intensity of Luc's firm stare. 'I don't think that's a good idea,' she said slowly.

'It's the only workable solution,' Luc replied, his tone turning brisk. 'I can't stay in Cornwall, and there's nothing really keeping you here anyway.'

Abby bristled. 'What about my job—and Grace?'

'Your job has to end,' Luc informed her brusquely. 'And Grace can visit if she means so much to you. You need looking after.'

'I'm not an invalid—'

'Not yet. But you're anaemic and exhausted, Abby, and you have a condition that requires some care. You must see the reason in this!' He paused, and when he spoke again his voice was careful, controlled. 'I accept that you do not wish to spend time with me, as it will undoubtedly be uncomfortable for us both. But, for the sake of our child, surely we can both look past this…discomfort and do what is necessary?'

He made it sound as if spending time together was the equivalent of taking a dose of particularly nasty medicine. Perhaps it was, to him.

It was that thought that made her determined not to go to France, as much as her heart leaped at the thought. As much as she wanted to. In the end it would be unbearable, living with Luc, being so near him and yet still so very far away.

'There have to be other options.'

'Let's name them, shall we?' Luc sat down in the chair next

to her bed and began to tick off on his fingers. 'You could go and stay with your mother?'

Abby shook her head. 'No, she's too busy.' The thought of spending her days in the little terraced house in Manchester, listening to her mother's lectures about how to resurrect her music career, was too awful an idea to contemplate.

'Your father, then.'

Again Abby shook her head. 'He's on tour.'

'Tour?'

She smiled. 'My retirement turned out to be the best thing for both of us. He turned back to his own music and was picked up by an agent. He's going on tour for the next few months. That's why I was in London, actually.'

'That's good news.'

'Yes.' But it meant she had no one to stay with, Abby thought despondently. It meant she had to depend on Luc.

'You could always hire a professional,' Luc said, and Abby stiffened.

'You mean a nurse? I told you, I'm not an invalid.'

'Indeed not.'

Abby pleated her cover restlessly between her fingers. 'Why, Luc?' she asked, her voice no more than a whisper. Luc didn't answer, and she forced herself to elaborate. 'Why are you doing this?' She looked up and met his shuttered gaze. 'Why do you care? You told me you didn't have any more to give. So why does it matter to you where I am or what I do?'

Her voice rose in a cry of naked despair. 'Or is it not about me at all, but the baby? Are you only doing this for the baby?' She wasn't sure why she felt the need to state it so plainly. She was virtually asking him to reject her, yet she needed to know. She needed to hear it from him.

Luc was silent for a long moment. He turned to stare out of the window, at the unending darkness of the night-shrouded sea. 'I made some grave mistakes in my life,' he finally said, his voice low, his words chosen carefully. 'I don't want to make them again.'

'Are you… Are you talking about your wife?'

'Suzanne.' The single word was spoken flatly, without emotion.

Suzanne; she had a name. She became more real to Abby then, a woman with a name and a story, and she wasn't sure she liked it. 'Suzanne?' she repeated, and then waited.

Luc, however, wasn't going to answer her question. 'Why not come to France, Abby?' he said, his voice gentle once more. 'You can relax, rest. I will do everything to make you comfortable.'

Except care. Except love her. He would be considerate, solicitous, but Abby didn't know if she could bear it. 'And what will I do in France?' she asked, sounding irritable, but unable to help it. 'Besides sit around all day, that is?'

Luc's mouth quirked in a half-smile. 'You could do the second thing you wanted.' Abby shook her head, not understanding. 'You could learn to cook.' She let out a little laugh of disbelief, and his smile widened. 'I already told you that I don't cook. It would be helpful, having someone to make the meals.'

'You probably have a housekeeper.'

'She does the laundry and cleaning only.'

Abby laughed again, suddenly glad that Luc wasn't going to let her feel sorry for herself. 'So, you want me to be your hired help?'

'Actually, no,' he told her, his face grave once more. 'I wasn't planning on paying you.'

Abby laughed for real this time, a delighted gurgle of sound. She leaned back against the pillows and closed her eyes, fighting a sudden helpless sorrow that followed on the heels of her happiness. *Don't make me fall in love with you.*

'Say yes, Abby,' Luc murmured. 'I want you there. I want you to come with me.'

Abby opened her eyes. Luc was gazing at her, his face softened by a smile. She could see the glint of stubble on his jaw and remembered how it felt against her own skin. She should say no. She knew that. There were other options, and she was in dangerous territory. Heartbreaking territory.

She should absolutely, one-hundred percent, say no.

'Yes,' she whispered.

CHAPTER TEN

THEY left for France the next day. As soon as Abby had given that one word of acceptance Luc had set plans into motion. She'd barely had time to pack a bag, notify her landlords and tell Grace she was leaving. Luc had smoothed it all over, hiring someone to replace her, finding a new tenant. Being rich, Abby thought a bit sourly, was like waving a magic wand. She'd had long enough now to know what it felt like *not* to be rich.

'Are you sure this is the right thing to do?' Grace had asked when Abby had gone to say goodbye. Grace's hands were covered in flour and her forehead was pleated in concern.

Abby shrugged. 'I'm not sure I have that many options. And I know Luc will take good care of me.'

'He's the father, isn't he?' Grace had said quietly, her eyes on the mound of bread dough she was kneading. 'He let Corner Cottage a few months ago—right around the time you fell pregnant, I suppose.'

'You're very good at putting two and two together,' Abby had told her. 'And getting four. Or, in this case,' she added wryly, patting her bump, 'three.'

'Did you know him before?'

Abby hesitated. Grace knew little of her previous life;

she'd known Abby had been a pianist, of course, but since she wasn't well acquainted with the music world it hadn't made much impact. Abby didn't feel like going into all the details now. 'Yes,' she said finally. 'A little.'

'Enough to go with him? To trust him?'

'I'd trust Luc with my life,' Abby replied, surprising herself with her own sincerity. She did trust Luc, with a heartfelt certainty. He was honest, he was caring, he was steadfast.

He just didn't love her. Couldn't.

'Then go with my good wishes,' Grace said, smiling a bit sadly. 'I'll miss you, Abby.'

'I'll miss you, too.' Abby hugged her friend, conscious of Grace's thin shoulder blades and fragile figure. 'I'm glad Luc found someone else to help you out.'

'I'd rather have you.'

'I'd rather be here, too,' Abby admitted. 'But I'll be back soon enough.'

Grace's smile was almost arch. 'Will you really?'

'Of course I will!' Abby returned. Yet even as she said the words she wondered to herself, *would she*? Luc had made it plain he saw no reason for her to stay in Cornwall. She'd said as much herself; this had been a respite, not a life.

So where was her new life—her baby's life—to be? Would Luc want her to stay in France, so he could be near? Just what was he expecting? What did he want?

What did *she* want?

'Anyway,' she told Grace firmly, 'I'll keep in touch.'

That afternoon Luc drove them out to a private airstrip near Exeter. Clouds scudded across an unfriendly grey sky as he parked the hired car and helped Abby board his private jet.

She gazed at the plane's sleek interior, the plush leather chairs, the mahogany coffee-table, the fresh flowers and stocked bar and slowly shook her head. 'Just how rich are you?'

'Rich enough.' Luc shrugged off his jacket and sat down,

beckoning Abby to join him. She sank into a seat across from him.

'What do you do for a living?' she asked, realizing she'd never bothered to ask such a mundane question before.

'I manage assets,' Luc replied.

'Whose?'

'Mine.'

One of the jet's staff came forward. *'Vous êtes prêt, Monsieur le Comte?'*

'Oui. Merci, Jacques.'

Abby bolted upright in her seat. '"Monsieur le Comte"?' she repeated incredulously. 'Are you a *count*?'

Luc shrugged. 'It means very little.'

'You're nobility?' Abby clarified, still disbelieving, and Luc gave a terse little nod. 'I thought all the noble titles went out with the French Revolution.'

'They did, but over the centuries several hundred have been reinstated. Obviously we have no real power, just the title.'

And the money, Abby filled in silently. And probably the land as well. 'So what is your full name, then?'

Luc paused. 'Jean-Luc Toussaint, Comte de Gévaudan,' he finally said, the words, the title, almost sounding distasteful.

The Count of Gévaudan; it sounded like something out of a story. A fairy tale. Abby shook her head slowly, lapsing into silence. It was just a little detail to Luc, but it made her realize how little she knew him, even if at times she felt like she knew him more than anyone else she'd ever known. She still didn't know the facts, the details. She also realized she had no idea where or what she was going to. She remembered back in Paris that Luc had told her he lived in the Languedoc. She knew no more.

'A count,' she finally said, turning back to look at him. 'Does that mean if our baby was a boy, he could have inherited?'

'Only if we were married,' Luc responded flatly, and Abby flushed.

Married. That, obviously, was never going to happen. Not that she even wanted it to. The last thing she'd agree to was some ghastly marriage of convenience simply for their child's sake, a loveless union...

Surely Luc didn't have such a thing in mind? No, of course not. She had a feeling *he* didn't want to be married, either.

She turned to stare out of the window as the plane began to taxi down the runway. Within minutes they were soaring through the sky, the dank clouds left far below them, so that bright azure stretched in every direction.

Jacques returned to serve them drinks, and Abby accepted an orange juice. She sipped it moodily while Luc spread some papers across his lap-tray, a cup of coffee growing cold by his elbow. She didn't know why it bothered her that he was clearly so immersed in work. He obviously had things to do, a life to live, and the last thing she wanted was to keep him from it.

She just wished she had something of her own. For a moment she longed to play piano, to feel the smooth, ivory keys under her fingers producing sound, making magic. She forced the feeling away. She leaned her head back against the seat and closed her eyes again, longing for the oblivion of sleep. Despite her physical fatigue, her nerves were too jumpy for her to doze or even to settle, and the minutes stretched into an hour without Luc even looking up once.

She should just get used to it, Abby supposed. Luc might want her to come to France, might want to take care of her, but apparently that didn't necessarily mean he wanted to talk to her.

Luc couldn't concentrate. He couldn't focus enough to even read the print on the papers spread before him, but he remained staring down at them with a deliberate intentness in an effort to give Abby some space.

She hadn't wanted to come to France; that had been plain enough last night. *He* shouldn't want her to come to France, and especially not to the Languedoc, where his memories were, where his heart was. He hadn't intended to bring her to the farmhouse; he kept it shut these days, along with the chateau. He avoided the entire region as much as he could. Yet some latent instinct had insisted that he bring Abby here. Home.

Yet what good could come of their continued relationship? What hope? The answer was obvious: a child. Only the child, innocent, untouched. Now that a child—his child—was involved, Luc knew he needed to have Abby in his life. He needed to be in hers. Even if it hurt them both.

For a moment he allowed himself to think of the child he might have had. He or she would have been three years old now if Suzanne's pregnancy had continued to term. It was nearly impossible to imagine what that life would look like now—a wife, a child, a home, a family. All things that had been denied him, all things he now never hoped to have, because he'd lost them once before. He'd as good as given them away.

Yet somehow, in a twist of fate or perhaps even providence, he was being given a second chance of sorts. A chance to be a father again.

And what about a husband? a sly inner voice asked. *What about Abby?*

He lifted his gaze from his papers to gaze at her covertly. She was staring out of the window, her expression distant and a little sad, the cool glass of juice pressed against one cheek. Her hair, carelessly tousled, lay in lustrous dark waves to her shoulders, and her eyes were wide and dark. She caught her full lower lip between her teeth and nibbled, a clear sign of anxiety.

Fresh guilt washed over Luc. He was the cause of that anxiety, no doubt. He should have stayed away from her completely, never have come to Cornwall to find her the first time. Yet even as he acknowledged this he knew he was tired of feeling guilty, tired of trying to find a way to redeem the past, atone for his sins.

To make it right.

He never could. No matter how well he might take care of Abby now, he'd already failed one woman.

He couldn't bring Suzanne back from the dead. He couldn't, as he'd told Abby months ago, turn back time.

And that, he determined, was why he would not fail Abby. He wouldn't let her down, because he wouldn't allow either of them the opportunity to be let down. It was the only way of keeping her safe.

The plane landed at a private airstrip near Avignon, and Luc had their bags transferred to a waiting luxury sedan. He slid into the driver's seat, with Abby next to him, and within minutes they were speeding down a narrow road running along the Rhône River. Already Abby felt herself relaxing under the deep blue sky. The air was warm and dry, scented with thyme and lavender. Fields and meadows stretched alongside the river in a patchwork of green, and in the distance Abby could see the craggy tops of the Pyrenees.

'How long a drive is it?' she asked.

'No more than thirty minutes. My house is just south of Pont-Saint-Esprit.'

They rode in silence, which was just as well, as Abby felt sleepy again and was content to sit there, drowsy from sunshine. Soon enough Luc turned the car off the main road to an even narrower track. Abby stirred herself to look out of the window with interest; they drove past a high stone-wall interrupted by ornate iron gates, the words *Chateau Mirabeau* worked into the iron in elegant scrollwork. The crenellated top of a turret was visible above the treeline. She glanced at Luc, to ask about the chateau, but then saw how tense he looked. His knuckles were white as he gripped the steering wheel, his jaw taut with strain. Curiosity bit at her, but she said nothing as a few minutes later Luc parked the car in front of a rambling stone farmhouse.

'It is a simple place,' he told her. 'But, I assure you, you will be comfortable.'

Abby could only nod, her throat suddenly tight. The farmhouse was just as she'd imagined on that long-ago night when she'd pictured Luc's home and thought she was being fanciful.

It was made of old, mellowed stone, with a red-tiled roof and brightly painted shutters. Abby wasn't sure she'd ever seen a more pleasant sight. Luc led the way to the old-fashioned Dutch door, swinging it open and ushering Abby inside.

Inside, the farmhouse had been renovated to create one large, airy space. The lounge area was scattered with comfortable sofas and chairs in front of a large stone fireplace. The kitchen looked like a perfect place to cook, with pale-oak cupboards and a smooth slate floor now dipped in sunshine. As Abby stepped in, a grey, cashmere-soft cat leapt from the shadows and, purring, wound its way around her ankles.

She laughed in delight and reached down to stroke the cat behind its ears.

'I hope you're not allergic?'

'No. I always wanted a pet. What's her name? Or *his* name, I suppose?'

'That one?' Luc squinted in concentration. 'That must be Sophie. Simone has black stripes.'

'There's another?' Abby reached down to scoop the cat into her arms and was rewarded with a deep, thrumming purr. 'I don't think I would have pegged you as a cat person.'

'I'm not,' Luc replied, his tone turning short. 'They're barn cats now, really.'

'They don't act like barn cats,' Abby said with a laugh. Sophie was lying docile in her arms, her tummy offered for Abby to scratch.

'They used to be quite spoiled,' Luc replied. His back was to her as he moved about the room, switching on lights. 'They'll wrap you around their paws, I'm sure.'

'Probably,' Abby agreed. She let Sophie go, conscious of a sudden coolness in the room, in the air between them. The cats used to be spoiled, Luc had said. By whom—his wife? It seemed likely, and it made Abby a little sad. What had his marriage been like? What had his wife been like? She didn't have the courage to ask, or even to hear the answers, yet she knew deep inside that she would never fully understand Luc until he told her.

If he ever told her.

'Where do I sleep?' she asked after a long, silent moment.

'There are three bedrooms upstairs. You may have whichever you prefer.'

'Which one is yours?' Abby asked, and then flushed to the roots of her hair. 'I mean, so I know not to pick that one.'

Luc turned around; his eyes were dark and shadowed. 'I usually sleep in the bedroom facing the back, but it doesn't matter.'

'You don't live here?' Abby asked. 'I mean, you make it sound—'

'I live here when I need to be in this area,' Luc said with a shrug. 'But mostly I travel for work.'

'Managing those assets?'

'Yes.'

'All right,' Abby said after a moment. 'I'll take a look.' She moved towards the narrow, curving stairs in the rear of the kitchen, and then after a second's hesitation scooped up the still-purring Sophie. She could use some pleasant company.

She picked the bedroom farthest from the one Luc used, a pleasant room with a wide double-bed, an old mahogany chest-of-drawers and a stunning view of the fields of lavender waving gently in the spring sunshine. Just as she'd imagined. It was eerie, how well she'd imagined this place, as if a part of her had *known*. She belonged here. It was a strange thought, an unsettling and even an unreasonable one, yet Abby felt it deeply in her bones, in her soul. This was home. At least, it *could* be, if things were different, if *Luc* were different...

Suppressing a sigh, she squinted in the sunlight as she gazed out of the window, making out the dark rooftops of what had to be the nearby chateau. Did it belong to Luc? If he really was a count, surely he had a chateau? Unless he had sold it. When they'd driven past, he'd seemed so tense. Had he lived there with his wife? Could he not bear to return now that she was gone? Although she was intensely curious, Abby knew she wouldn't ask. She didn't think she was ready for the answers.

Back downstairs Luc was already sorting through post at the kitchen table, scanning the letters with an air of deliberate concentration. He barely glanced up when Abby reappeared in the stairwell. 'You should rest this afternoon. Tomorrow we'll go to Pont-Saint-Esprit for supplies.'

'All right,' Abby agreed, and, a bit disconsolately, she wandered back upstairs. She was tired, but she didn't feel like sleeping. She wanted to explore, to talk, to discover more about the man she was half-falling in love with. *Half*— because she didn't *know* the other half. And she had no good way of finding out.

The rest of the day passed slowly enough. Abby rested, and then Luc prepared a meal of pasta and tinned sauce which they ate in the kitchen as the sun slowly set over the mountains, casting long, golden rays across the slate floor.

'I really shall have to learn to cook,' Abby teased, and Luc shrugged.

'Only if you want to.'

There could be no denying, Abby thought as she helped with the washing up after their meal, that since coming to France Luc had shut himself up like a box. Gone was the laughter lurking in his eyes, the hint of a smile. The darkness Abby had always sensed underneath had come to the fore, taking over his countenance like a malevolent shadow. He barely spoke, and as soon as possible he retreated to what she suspected was both a sanctuary and a defence: his work.

The next day was bright and sunny, the air dry and warm and scented with lavender as they headed into town to buy the promised supplies.

'It's market day,' Luc said, 'so there should be plenty of fresh fruit and vegetables.'

Abby nodded. She was looking forward to getting out and seeing a bit more of the countryside, and escaping the increasingly grim mood of the farmhouse. If she'd known how Luc would act here, she never would have come to France, she thought sourly, even as she recognized her other options were severely limited.

They drove in silence along the main road into town. The meadows ran parallel to the gently flowing Rhône, and they drove over the ancient stone bridge with its many arches that led into the town.

Luc parked near the centre, and soon they were wandering down cobbled streets, peeking into dusty little shops and market stalls with their colourful awnings.

Abby was enchanted, enthralled by the glass bottles of locally produced olive oil, the dishes of tapenade, the barrels of oranges and ropes of garlic and onions. She soon filled a basket that Luc carried; he glanced at the various wrapped packages with an arched eyebrow.

'You are planning to cook with this, I presume?'

'Of course,' Abby replied, then added a bit sheepishly, 'but I suppose I'll need a cookbook.'

'There are several at the farmhouse,' Luc told her. 'In French, of course, but that shouldn't be a problem, should it?'

'*Bien sûr, non,*' Abby replied a bit flippantly, and was rewarded with the faintest flicker of a smile. She paused by a selection of wines, scanning the labels then coming up short. 'Chateau Mirabeau,' she read on one bottle of red. 'But that's the place right near us.'

'Indeed.' Luc looked almost bored, and Abby glanced around, suddenly noticing the way the wine merchant hovered near them, practically bowing to Luc, his hands clasped before him. Of course, he reocognized Luc. If Luc was the local nobility, everyone must recognize him. Everyone must wonder what he was doing with her. Perhaps they'd known his wife.

Suddenly Abby became conscious of the covert, sideways glances, the ripple of murmurs in the market. She'd been so enchanted by everything she hadn't noticed at first, yet now she felt exposed, obvious. She put the bottle back with a clatter and turned to Luc.

'I suppose we should go.'

'You have everything you need?'

'Yes, and I…I'm getting tired.' She knew that would make Luc hurry, and sure enough he was soon hustling them back to the car. Abby sank into the passenger seat with relief. She didn't know why the stares and whispers of the crowd had bothered her so much—she was certainly used to some amount of public attention.

Just not like this, she thought. Because of things she didn't know, a past she didn't understand. She turned to Luc. He was driving, staring straight ahead, his hands tight on the steering wheel. 'People knew you.' He shrugged. 'They all recognized you,' she pressed. 'But you said you don't really live here.' Luc still said nothing, and Abby forced herself to continue. 'Did you live here once? With—with Suzanne?'

'Yes.'

'How did she die?'

'A car accident.' He gestured to the road, to the river flowing sluggishly by. 'Right near here, a completely straight stretch.' His voice was strained, almost cold, and it kept Abby from saying anything more; surely it hid a grief too deep and raw to acknowledge? He glanced at her, his eyes narrowed, although Abby saw a certain weariness etched into his features. 'Why are you asking these questions, Abby?'

'Because I want to know. I need to know, Luc. There is so much I don't know about you.'

Luc turned back to gaze at the road, and the sorrowful silence stretched between them. 'Maybe it's better that way,' he said finally.

Abby added silently, *only if we don't have a future.*

That afternoon, while Luc worked in his study, Abby set up in the kitchen. She had an old, worn cookbook propped in front of her and all her market-place purchases scattered on the oak worktop. She was going to make dinner.

'Hot radishes with salted liver,' she read. 'Snails with nettles.' She made a face. This was French cooking? She turned a page and settled on a simple cassoulet, as she had most of the ingredients and the recipe looked relatively simple—plonk in a pot and stir.

The room was soon filled with a variety of tempting aromas: oregano, thyme, the rich scent of red wine heavy on the air. The late-afternoon sunlight poured through the windows, and as Abby stirred the large cast-iron pot Sophie came in, purring plaintively as she wound around her ankles.

'Don't beg,' Abby told the cat. 'It's not polite.'

The cat rubbed against her calf, and laughingly Abby gave

her a titbit of food. Everything was so perfect, she thought with a sigh. The food, the sunshine, the drowsy, warm air, even the cat. It was all part of her fantasy of a home, a life, and yet she couldn't be satisfied because she knew it wouldn't last. It was false, because the man at the centre of the fantasy didn't love her. Didn't, apparently, even want to be with her.

'Stop it, Abby,' she told herself. 'It's not going to happen, so just forget it.'

'What's not going to happen?' Abby looked up, flushing, to see Luc in the kitchen doorway, one shoulder propped against the frame. 'Who were you talking to? The cat?'

'Myself, actually,' she replied as she put the lid on the pot. 'It's a habit of mine.'

'Is it?'

'There hasn't always been someone else to talk to,' Abby said pointedly, and Luc gave an apologetic shrug—at least that was what Abby hoped it was.

'I'm sorry, I haven't been here in some months, and I needed to deal with some work.'

'If I had a place like this, I'd stay here for ever,' Abby said, meaning to be flippant, but it came out far too sincerely. Luc stilled.

'Would you?' he asked quietly and Abby hurried to explain.

'I only meant it's so relaxing here,' she said, her head bent as she wrung out a dish cloth and began to swipe at the worktop with a little too much vigour.

'I'm glad you think so. That was my hope in bringing you here.'

'So.' Abby wrung the cloth out again and hung it by the sink to dry. 'If you haven't been here, where have you been?'

'Paris, mostly.'

'Paris?' How could a single word conjure so many memories? They poured through her as sweet as honey, yet with a fiery power that made her almost sway. 'Do you stay at the hotel?' She bit her lip, wishing she hadn't asked that question. It had slipped out, part of the memory. She could almost feel the crisp bite of champagne on her tongue, the languorous desire running through her veins.

'No,' Luc said after a moment. 'I stay somewhere else.'

'Do you have a flat?'

'I did.' He paused again. 'I sold it.'

'Why?'

He shrugged, a restless movement, and glanced at the pot she was stirring. 'That smells delicious. What is it?'

Abby sighed, relegating her unanswered question to being just another thing about Luc she neither knew nor understood. 'Cassoulet. I decided not to try the snails with nettles.'

Luc's mouth curved into a smile that had Abby's insides flip-flopping in response. 'Too bad we didn't pick up any snails at the market. They're very good when they're fresh, even if they are, as you once said, *snails*.'

'I'll trust you on that one.' His low chuckle seemed to wind its way around her soul, seducing her heart. She turned to stir the cassoulet, to distract her body from its treacherous yearnings. Then she felt another flip-flop, only this one was even stronger. 'Oh!'

'Abby, what? Are you all right?'

'Yes.' Abby pressed her hand against her bump. 'The baby…she kicked me! I felt it!' She laughed, a sound of incredulous joy. 'There! She did it again.'

'Can I…?'

'Yes, yes.' Buoyed by excitement, Abby reached for his hand and pressed it against her middle. They waited in silent, tense expectation for a moment before the baby obliged and kicked again, right into Luc's palm. He laughed aloud. 'Amazing, isn't it?' Abby shook her head, unable to keep the ridiculously wide grin off her face. 'She's really in there.'

'She is.' Luc did not take his hand from her bump, and as Abby looked up at him, their gazes locking, the moment stretched between them in an intimate silence. She felt the breath dry in her throat and her heart begin to beat with heavy, deliberate thuds. She wanted that moment to last for ever, to be cocooned in the shared miracle of their child, the warmth of Luc's hand against her stomach. This feeling that anything was possible, that the world—life and love—was theirs for the taking, the enjoying. The sharing.

'Luc,' she breathed, and didn't dare to say any more. He said nothing, and for a moment Abby rested and even reveled in the moment, fragile as it was. She closed her eyes, and raised her hand to cover Luc's, but before their fingers touched he moved his hand and stepped away.

'I need to make some calls before dinner,' he said, his tone abrupt, and before Abby could even make a reply he'd left the room.

Luc walked blindly to his study where he stood still, his hands braced flat on his desk as he drew in deep lungfuls of air, almost as if he'd just finished a sprint.

He was dizzy with emotion from that brief moment with Abby, the memory of her hand on his; the baby's feather-light kicks dancing on his palm still created little aftershocks of awareness, electrifying his soul. He'd felt happy, hopeful, alive, and it amazed him. He'd *felt*—even stronger than ever before. His heart and body had come to life, reawakening his senses. His soul.

It was wonderful. It was terrifying. He closed his eyes and willed his heart to slow. He didn't like the fear that followed the joy; it crept into him and settled coldly in his bones. When you felt so much, you could lose so much.

For a moment he was back on that stretch of road—the wrecked car wrapped around a tree, the smell of fire and death thick in the air, futility and powerlessness swamping him.

He couldn't lose Abby. He couldn't—yet what was there to lose? They weren't married; they weren't even lovers any more. She'd come here simply for the sake of her child; he needed to remember that. He needed to keep his distance, keep from caring or letting her care.

It was too frightening, too dangerous for them both.

Luc didn't reappear in the kitchen until Abby was ladling the cassoulet into heavy ceramic bowls. The sky was dark with gathering shadows. She looked up as he approached, summoning a smile.

'I hope you're hungry. I seem to have made enough for an army.'

Luc didn't answer. He sat down and slid a slim, black phone across the table. Abby's fingers curled around it automatically. 'I'll be busy with work the next little while,' he said. 'But you can contact me in an emergency. I programmed my number into the phone.'

'I see.' Abby glanced down at the phone, a sure sign if there ever was one of Luc's emotional withdrawal. Yet what she expected? Back in Cornwall, she'd wanted him to leave her alone. Now that he was, Abby wondered if she'd fooled herself. Did she still want more from Luc? Had she come to France secretly hoping for a second or third chance? Was she really that self-deceiving and naïve? 'Thank you,' she said finally, and slid the phone into her pocket.

They ate in near silence, and soon after the meal Luc excused himself to return to his study. Abby made herself a cup of coffee and wandered out to the terrace behind the kitchen. The air was cool, the wind rattling in the olive trees, the sky inky-black and spangled with stars. Abby sighed deeply, breathing in the dry, dusty air. The gently rolling hills and meadows seemed to stretch out endlessly in front of her, dotted with the occasional olive or plane tree. In the distance she could see the towers of what must be Chateau Mirabeau, dark and silent under the moon. Perhaps she would explore the countryside tomorrow, Abby thought a bit disconsolately. Wander over to the chateau and see who lived there, if anyone. There wasn't much else to do.

She took a sip of her now-lukewarm coffee and let the night's cooling air settle over her. With a sudden, sharp pang of longing she wished things could be different. She wished she could return inside and pop her head around Luc's study door, tease him away from his work so they could sit here together, counting the stars. Or perhaps they would go right upstairs, to the wide, pine bed with its fluffy mattress and duvet and put it to good use...

The fantasy she spun for herself seemed so real, so possible, that Abby almost had to restrain herself from acting upon it. Luc was sending clear signals that he did not want to get emotionally involved. He'd been sending those signals for a year now, so why couldn't she accept them? Why did she still want more?

Because, Abby acknowledged, she wasn't satisfied. She was still in Luc's life, even if she wasn't involved in it. She didn't understand his past, the secrets he kept, the suffering he bore like a physical burden, weighing him down, reflected in the shadows in his eyes. She wanted to know. She wanted to understand.

And, yes, she acknowledged starkly, even as a little seed of hope inside her refused to die, she wanted more. She just didn't know if she would ever get it.

CHAPTER ELEVEN

Luc was as good as his word and left soon after a breakfast of coffee and rolls, telling Abby that he was touring offices nearby but that he could be home within minutes if needed.

'For an emergency?' Abby clarified, and he gave a tiny shrug as if to say 'of course'. Then he was gone.

She tidied up the kitchen before slipping into her one pair of maternity jeans—the waistbands of her normal clothes were by mow much too tight—a long-sleeved tee-shirt, a pair of sturdy hiking boots and headed outside.

The air was dry and fresh, the sun shining benevolently on the world, and a slight breeze ruffled Abby's hair and kept her from getting too hot. It was a perfect day for a walk.

She walked along the road for a while, past olive groves and rolling meadows, enjoying the chatter of birds above her, the sighing of the wind through the plane trees. Only one car passed her the entire time she walked, and the driver honked his horn in friendly salutation. Abby waved back, her spirits lifting slightly now that she was away from the increasingly oppressive atmosphere of the farmhouse.

Within a quarter of an hour she'd made her way to the ornate iron gates of Chateau Mirabeau; she acknowledged as she stood in front of them that this had been her destination all along. The gates were locked, and the wall on either side of them was at least six feet high of weathered, crumbling stone. There was no way in.

Not that she should go snooping around, Abby told herself. Someone probably lived there, some reclusive movie star or tycoon who would call the police if he saw someone skulking out in his garden.

Yet she was curious, intensely curious, drawn to this building in a way she couldn't even explain, yet somehow feeling as if she needed to see it. Uselessly she rattled the gates, the lock banging loudly against the iron, and then to her surprise the lock dropped to the ground. It was rusted, she saw instantly. The gate swung open, its hinges squeaking in protest, and Abby stepped inside.

The gravel drive up to the chateau was choked with weeds; the trees and shrubs on either side hung over it, nearly cloaking the lane in darkness, desperately needing to be cut back.

Abby walked up the twisting drive practically on her tiptoes, afraid she might disturb someone, although it became increasingly clear that no one lived here. The chateau was shrouded in neglect.

The drive snaked through the trees before opening up to a stunning vista of the building—a palace, really, for the chateau was certainly palatial. Towers flanked two long rows of windows now shuttered against the sun; Abby counted twenty-eight before she stopped.

She approached the house gingerly, coming to the front door and resting her hand on the heavy, bronze knob, warm from the sun, knowing before she tried that it wouldn't turn. Of course it wouldn't; whoever owned this place wouldn't leave it unlocked. Still, she circled the chateau, which took some time, picking her way along the terraces in the back which overlooked a splendid panorama of formal gardens, fountains and crumbling Roman aquaducts, all the while looking for another door, or even a broken window. There was nothing. She peered through the slats of a shutter, only to glimpse a salon full of dust sheets.

Why was she trying to break into this place? Abby wondered. What could she possibly find here? Shaking her head, now disappointed, tired, and hot, she finally returned the way she had come, picking her way through the weeds and then back along the hot, dusty road to the farmhouse.

She slept most of the afternoon, waking only when she heard the door open and footfalls downstairs. It was nearing supper time, and Luc had finally returned.

'I'm sorry I didn't make any supper,' she said as she came downstairs. Luc was standing by the stove, sorting through some post. 'I'm not earning my keep, am I?'

He looked up, his gaze meeting hers, seeming to light on her, warmly and openly, before it turned cool and blank once more. 'That's not why you're here.'

'Mmm.' Abby went to the fridge to retrieve the leftover cassoulet. That would have to do for dinner. 'I wonder why I *am* here.'

'To rest and relax and keep our child safe,' Luc replied, his tone turning a little sharp. 'Why else?'

Why else, indeed? Abby thought sourly. One day into her enforced exile and she was already feeling restless, picking fights. 'I walked over to the chateau today,' she said after a moment, and didn't think she imagined the tension that suddenly coiled through the room, emanating from Luc's stiff body.

'Oh?' he said, tossing a letter aside.

'Yes. It's beautiful, if a bit neglected. Why does no one live there?'

'I thought the gates were locked.'

Abby shrugged aside the question even as she wondered how Luc knew. He spoke of the chateau with a certain possessive knowledge. 'I managed to see a bit. It all looks terribly overgrown.'

'I suppose it is.'

'Do you know who lives there?' Luc paused, and Abby saw a telling hesitation shadow his eyes. 'Does the chateau belong to your family?' she asked quietly. 'If you're the local nobility, it makes sense.'

'Yes, it does,' Luc replied tersely, his tone final. 'But I choose not to live there. I find the farmhouse suitable for my needs.'

'Except you don't normally live here, either.'

He shrugged. 'I'm a busy man, Abby.'

'Obviously.' She took a breath, needing the courage to continue. 'Obviously too busy for me. Although, I can't help but wonder if you're just trying to avoid me.'

He stilled before slowly turning to face her. 'Why would I do that?'

'I don't know, Luc. Maybe you should tell me.'

'I'm not interested in some kind of amateur psychoanalysis.'

'I wasn't aware I was giving it,' Abby retorted. 'But, now that you mention it, maybe I should give it a try. Why did you invite me here, Luc, if you're going to ignore me? I could call 999 as easily in Cornwall as I could reach you.' She took a breath; it hurt her lungs. 'There's no real reason for me to be here, is there?'

His mouth tightened, his nostrils flaring. 'That's not true.'

'I thought you wanted to be involved,' Abby continued. 'In our baby's life, if not mine. But I'm realizing that can't really work. For either of us.'

'Abby—'

'What do you want from me?' she demanded, her voice raw, pleading. 'I wish you'd just leave me alone—stay out of my life completely—rather than provide all these half-measures. You wanted me to come to France, but now you're virtually ignoring me!'

'I'm sorry.' Luc's face was shuttered, his mouth tightly pursed. 'I thought I made it clear, what you could expect from me.' He spoke flatly, unemotionally, and somehow that hurt too.

'You mean, nothing?' Abby said, half-sarcastically, and Luke didn't respond.

'I see.' She swiped at a stray tear and forced herself to nod. She shouldn't be surprised; Luc had made it clear. It was her own wayward heart that kept hoping for more. 'Well, maybe it's just all these pregnancy hormones that are making me feel so emotional.'

Luc inclined his head in acknowledgement; clearly he didn't want to discuss it. 'I'll just clear a few things from my desk,' he murmured, and miserably Abby watched him retreat from her once more.

The next day she found herself alone again. The sky was a bright azure, the sun shining once more. She spent the morning in the kitchen attempting another recipe—this time a simple pasta dish—but realized belatedly she was missing some rather important ingredients: like pasta.

The sun beckoned enticingly and Abby decided to escape the confines of the farmhouse once more. Funny how she longed to leave it, for when she'd first arrived it had felt so welcoming, like a home. Now it felt like a prison.

She slipped on her jacket and headed outside, only to pause by the front door. Lying on top of a shelf next to a bunch of coat-hooks was a heavy, iron key, old and a bit rusted. Abby picked it up, thoughtfully turning it over in her hands, before she slipped it into the pocket of her coat.

She walked with quick purpose to her destination; the gates of the chateau were closed but thankfully still unlocked. Abby slipped between them and hurried up the shadowy drive to the front door of the chateau.

The key was slippery in her hand and yet, like in the kind

of fairy tale she'd believed to be false, it fitted snugly in the lock; after only a second's protest it turned, the squeaky sound seeming to echo in the silence. With the tip of her fingers Abby pushed the door open, and it swung inwards.

She stepped into the gloom of the central foyer; sunlight filtered from between the cracks of the shuttered windows and illuminated the dust motes dancing through the air. The chateau was utterly silent save for the drumming of Abby's heart. She blinked several times to accustom her eyes to the gloom, noticing the ghostly shapes of furniture shrouded in dust sheets. She took a few cautious steps into one of the main salons leading off from the foyer. Her feet when she walked gave up little puffs of dust.

She lifted one of the sheets away from a table, which revealed burnished wood inlaid with marble. It was an exquisite antique, and she suspected the whole chateau was full of them. Why was no one living here? Why wasn't *Luc* living here?

She walked through several of the main chambers, peeking under a few dust sheets, amazed at how empty and abandoned the entire place was. She should leave, she knew. She had no right to be here, to snoop and spy. Yet somehow she couldn't make herself go.

The clue, the key to Luc's life—his past life—was here. If he wouldn't tell her, perhaps she could find out on her own.

The rooms were silent, seemingly filled with ghosts who offered no explanations.

Then she came to the last of the formal rooms on the ground floor, its shuttered French doors led out to the terrace. Like all the others, its furniture was covered in dust sheets, yet one item gave away its nature even under such a shroud.

It was a grand piano.

Slowly Abby moved into the room. With one hand she reached out and pulled the sheet from the instrument; it came away in a whisper of a sound. The piano was beautiful. She recognized it as an Erard, an antique that had probably been in this family for a hundred years or more. The outside was heavily decorated with gilt, a work of art in itself. Slowly she eased the cover off the keys, not even sure why she was doing this. The piano would undoubtedly be badly out of tune, yet even so…

Her fingers hovered over the keys. She hadn't played piano in a year, hadn't *touched* a piano in a year. It was an unfathomably long time for someone who had played piano every day for several hours since she was five years old. She took a breath and then let her fingers ripple over the keys. Her fingers felt stiff, and the sound was out of tune, warbling disconsolately through the empty room, making Abby laugh a little. Something had loosened inside her when she'd touched those keys; she hadn't realized how tightly she'd been holding onto it until it was gone. Slowly, without even thinking about what she was doing, she began to play the *Appassionata*.

The gates were open, the lock dangling rusted and broken, as Luc pulled up to Chateau Mirabeau. He parked the car, his heart thudding with hard, heavy beats as he stared at the shadowy drive. He hadn't even looked upon the chateau for more than a year; he certainly hadn't been inside.

Ten minutes ago his security firm had rung him, saying the security system had picked up a person in the chateau. 'No signs of a break-in, but we just wanted to check,' the head of the firm, Eric, had told him.

'It's fine,' Luc replied tersely. 'There's no break-in.' For he knew just who had entered the chateau, who had been asking questions, who had undoubtedly found the key he'd left at the farmhouse for emergencies, who was snooping and prying into the past he longed to be forgotten. Erased.

Abby.

He slammed out of the car and walked up the drive, the gravel crunching under his feet. He hesitated briefly on the marble steps to the front entrance; the door was ajar. The last time he'd crossed that threshold he'd been running away, escaping the damning truth he'd found in Suzanne's letters:

I'm so unhappy…I never thought it would be like this…I want to escape…

And she had escaped, in the most final way possible.

He drew in a shuddering breath and stepped through the doorway. The foyer was full of muted sunlight filtering through the shuttered windows and illuminating the thick layer of dust that covered every beautiful surface. Luc let his fingers trail through the dust on the once-polished mahogany banister, remembering its burnished glow. This home had been his pride, his joy, his obsession.

Now it lay in near ruin, and by his own hand. He'd forbidden anyone to come to the chateau, to maintain or clean it. He supposed he'd wanted it to moulder, a form of self-punishment. Even now, gazing around at the shrouded rooms, he felt a stab of pain. How he'd loved this place. It hurt to see it like this.

And somewhere in this mausoleum of memories was Abby. He walked down the main hallway, past several salons, glancing in each one yet knowing, sensing, that Abby was not in any of them.

Then he heard it: music. Not just any music, but the most beautiful music of all, *Appassionata* played on a terribly out-of-tune piano yet recognizable nonetheless.

Luc walked like a man in a trance towards the music room. He paused in the doorway, his heart contracting. Abby stood at the piano, her body illuminated by the late-afternoon sunlight filtering through the shutters, her head bent, her hair a glossy, dark waterfall as she played. There was a look of reverence on her face.

Even amidst the dust and decay, even with the chateau no more than a pale shadow of what it had once been, Luc liked seeing Abby there. She looked right; she fit. And the music caused an ache to start deep inside him, an ache that had already been there, always been there, but which he could only acknowledge now.

The numbness fell away; he *felt*. His defences were crumbling; Abby slipped under them time and time again. It was getting harder to hold onto the numbness. Now he felt longing and fear and, most frighteningly of all, something all too terribly close to love.

Gritting his teeth, he shook his head, as if he could physically rid himself of the cascade of sensations, and stepped inside the room.

'What in God's name are you doing?'

Abby froze. Slowly she turned to face the doorway where Luc stood, his chest heaving, his eyes blazing blue fire.

'I was playing the piano,' she said after a long, tense moment. She tried to laugh, and didn't quite succeed. She didn't think she'd ever seen Luc look so angry. She stepped back from the piano, her fingers vibrating with memory, her heart singing. It had felt good to play, and the realization was one of wonderful relief.

Luc strode into the room, unamused, radiating a quiet, deadly fury. 'How did you get in here?'

'You left the key by the back door. How did you find me?'

'Do you think a place like this isn't armed?'

Abby stared at him blankly. *'Armed?'*

'Security!' Luc bit out. 'As soon as you opened the door, a security alarm went off. It goes directly to the security firm, and they rang me to check I hadn't set it off accidentally.'

Abby's eyes widened. 'I didn't hear anything.'

'You're not meant to. It's silent. The police would have been here in five minutes if I hadn't called them off.'

He looked so angry, Abby thought, yet frightened too. She wondered why. 'Why did you call them off? How did you know it was me?'

'You were asking questions about the chateau last night, and I know you well enough to realize you wouldn't leave it at that.' He smiled tightly. 'And I was right, wasn't I?'

'I was curious,' Abby said quietly. 'It could be so beautiful. Why is it all shut up?'

'I told you last night,' he said after a long moment. He glanced around the room, suddenly looking hunted, haunted. Abby suppressed the urge to walk over and wrap her arms around him. Despite his angry energy, he looked like a man in need of comfort. 'I don't want to live here.'

'Did you ever live here?'

He continued to survey the room; the sunlight slanted through the shutters, creating dusty bars of light on the parquet floor. 'I grew up here.'

Abby glanced back at the piano. There were ghosts in this room, she thought, ghosts and memories. Her own memories haunted her, memories of a life dedicated to professional playing when she didn't even know if that was what she'd ever wanted, yet she couldn't imagine a life without music. She touched the keys again and Luc winced.

'It's very out of tune,' he said flatly.

'Yes, I don't think I've ever played such a badly tuned piano before.'

'You must have played on some of the greatest pianos ever made.'

'Yes.' Impulsively she played the first few bars of the *Apassionata* once more. Even out of tune, the sound was both lovely and haunting. The music seemed to wrap around them, seductive and heavy with memories. Luc stilled. Abby stepped away from the piano, suddenly shaken.

'Do you miss it?' he asked quietly.

'I miss the music.' She took a breath, deciding to be honest. 'The joy.' She turned to him. 'Do you?'

'Miss what?'

'This. Her.' Abby gestured to the chateau generally, yet the arc of her arm encompassed so much more. 'We've both lived past lives, Luc. Do you miss it? Is that why you shut everything up, why you never talk about it?' Her voice took on a raw, pleading edge. 'Because you miss it so much?'

He didn't answer. The silence seemed to stretch endlessly between them, filled with unspoken thoughts, regrets, memories. Abby turned back to the piano and picked out a few dissonant notes. They fell into the dust and stillness, and died away completely before Luc spoke.

'No, I don't miss it.' He paused, his gaze shadowed, distant. 'I suppose that's what I regret.'

It took Abby a moment to understand. '*Not* missing it?'

'If you're thinking I can't give you what you need because I'm mourning my wife, Abby, then you couldn't be more wrong,' Luc stated with an almost clinical detachment, yet when he finished he drew in a shuddering breath; Abby could feel the torrent of regret and sorrow coursing through him.

'Then why?' she asked quietly, her fingers still stroking the smooth ivory of the piano keys. 'Why are you the way you are, Luc? What happened to make you regret so much?'

'I thought—' Luc broke off, shaking his head. Abby waited. After a moment he walked to the French windows, shuttered against the sunlight, and in one deft movement unlocked the window and thrust open the shutter. Late-afternoon sunlight streamed in, making Abby blink. The view from the window was magnificent; the terrace led to landscaped albeit overgrown gardens that descended in a rolling meadow straight to the Rhône. On the other side of the river she could see the twisted trunks of an olive grove, and further away still a vineyard.

'I love this place,' Luc said in a low voice, and somehow it seemed as if this was part of the explanation, the story. 'I've always loved it. I suppose it's in my blood.'

'It's been in your family for generations?' Abby surmised, and Luc nodded.

'Four hundred years.' He lapsed into silence, still gazing out at his gardens, his property, his inheritance, his legacy. His very life. After a moment Abby left the piano, taking a step towards him. She stopped when Luc spoke again.

'My father died when I was eleven. It was a heart attack, very sudden.' He stopped abruptly, his face shuttered, and Abby's heart ached for such a loss.

'I'm sorry.'

'I miss him.' He spoke quietly, giving a little shake of his head. 'He was a good man.' He paused, and when he resumed his voice was stiff again, as if reciting mere, stale facts. 'As it happened, he hadn't had the opportunity to put his affairs in order. My mother did the best she could, but with a corrupt estate-manager, and the myriad responsibilities of owning such a vast estate, things fell into disrepair.' He gave a little shrug. 'I'm telling you this so you can understand why, *who*, I am. That is what you wanted, yes?'

'Yes,' Abby whispered.

'I watched Chateau Mirabeau grow more decrepit, our holdings and investments shrink and fail; if my father had been alive, he would have despaired. But then, if he'd been alive, it would not have happened.' He sighed, suddenly weary.

'As it was, I was only a boy and powerless to do anything. My mother and sisters did not concern themselves too much, as long as they had what they needed, which they did. We were never destitute.' He sighed again and rubbed a hand over his face. 'But it burned within me. I couldn't wait to gain back all we had lost. It was all I could think of, all I ever cared about.' Another pause, and then he amended, 'All I let myself care about, I suppose.'

A telling remark, Abby thought. Was it still all he let himself care about? Was his unwillingness to care for her a *choice*?

'When I was nineteen,' Luc continued, 'I took control of the estate, the vineyards, all of Toussaint Holdings. Of course, by that time, there wasn't as much left as one might have wished. But I spent the next ten years devoted to returning my family's inheritance back to its former glory. It became an *obsession*.' He spoke the word as though it were a confession, with contempt. Abby simply waited, saying nothing. 'I was successful, after a time, but it was never enough. I always wanted—' He paused. 'It always seemed like there was more to do, more to make secure. More to achieve.'

He turned to Abby, a grim smile twisting his features. 'Suzanne fit into all these plans. She was from a neighbouring family, eligible, suitable. I'd known her since infancy. I thought she'd make the perfect bride.'

A checklist, Abby thought, neatly ticked. 'And?' she asked when it didn't seem like he was going to continue.

'And she did, on paper. But I didn't know...' He shook his head. 'I didn't realize the cost to her,' he finally said. He gave a laugh, harsh and unforgiving. 'I thought we were happy, or at least content. Or maybe I didn't, but I never even let myself think too much about it. About her.'

'Weren't you happy?' Abby whispered.

Luc shook his head. 'Suzanne had a miscarriage early in our marriage. She was only a few weeks' pregnant, but it nearly destroyed her. I didn't even appreciate how much, she hid it so well. Or perhaps I just didn't bother to look.' He turned away. 'I was saddened too, of course,' he continued after a moment. 'But I assumed there would be other children.' For a moment he glanced at Abby, and her hand stole inadvertently to her bump: *the other child*. His. Hers.

Luc gave a shrug, spreading his hands. 'What can I say that will excuse my behaviour? I buried myself in work and left her here, to act as chatelaine. She hated the role. She was lonely, overwhelmed…' He trailed off. 'I didn't even know it, but she'd been prescribed antidepressants. No one told me.' He shook his head. 'I was blind to it all, wilfully blind, too wrapped up in the kingdom I was trying to build—and for what?'

He turned back to the view, his hands shoved deep in his pockets, his body radiating tension and a sorrowful anger.

'It sounds as if she was trying to hide her illness,' Abby said quietly. 'Surely it wasn't your fault?'

'How can you say it wasn't my fault?' Luc demanded. 'Suzanne was my wife—she was only twenty years old when we married. She was my responsibility, and I should have been able to see! I didn't even realize she knew—'

'Knew what?'

He shook his head impatiently, spitting out the words. 'That I didn't love her. I was fond of her, of course, and I thought she'd make a suitable wife. But she needed to be loved, and I couldn't provide that for her.' His voice was little more than an aching whisper. 'Sometimes I wonder if that was why…' He broke off, pressing his lips together in a hard line.

Abby waited, knowing the words would come when Luc was able to say them. 'Why she had the car accident,' Luc said. She had to strain to hear his words. 'I don't know where she was going; she never drove anywhere. The road was perfectly straight, yet she just veered off into the river.' He stopped again, almost gasping before he tightened his lips once more; his whole face closed in on itself, wiped clean of the agony Abby knew he must still feel inside.

'You think she did it on purpose,' she said quietly, and Luc gave a terse nod.

'It was judged to be an accident—but who knows? Who really knows?'

The not knowing would be the worst, Abby thought with a rush of sorrow. The endless wondering. Yet, looking at Luc now, his shoulders bowed with suffering and guilt, she knew he had taken too much onto himself. He'd taken all of it, assumed complete responsibility for Suzanne's life—and death—just as he'd been doing with hers. No wonder he felt he had nothing more to give, Abby thought sadly. Loving someone was too hard when you made yourself utterly responsible for her happiness.

'You can't blame yourself for someone else's life, Luc,' Abby said gently. 'Or for their sorrow or happiness. Even if you were blind to what Suzanne was feeling, or too obsessed with work. You can take responsibility for your own actions, but not for someone else's.' Luc shook his head, an instinctive movement, and Abby continued. 'You know, that's something I've come to realize myself. I was living my life for my father, because playing piano professionally was his dream, not mine. I made it mine to please him, please everyone, and lost myself in the process. I lost the joy of music I'd always had.' Even now the confession caused an ache of longing within her, and she glanced at the piano, now cast in shadow.

'But you play so beautifully.'

'And I love playing,' Abby agreed with a sad smile. 'Just perhaps not in a concert hall. Not to the exclusion of everything else. And I can't make my father happy by playing piano; I can't give him his dream. I think he's finally acknowledged that too; we're finally living our own lives.' She tried to smile, but there was too much pain and sorrow for her to do more than blink back the tears she longed to shed for both of them.

He took a step towards her. 'Why don't you hate me?' he asked in a low voice.

'Hate you?' Abby repeated softly. 'Why would I hate you? *How* could I hate you?'

'After everything I've just said, after everything I've done.' He spread his hands wide. 'I walked away from you, Abby, because I was afraid. And selfish. There was nothing more I wanted to do than stay with you that night, and wake up with you in the morning. Every morning.' He was walking straight towards her, so close that Abby found herself leaning back against the gilded edge of the piano, suddenly breathless.

'Why?' she whispered. 'Why did you leave, then?'

'That day…' He paused, his features twisting in painful memory. 'That afternoon I was sorting through some papers here. I found some letters of Suzanne's—letters she'd written to herself, a journal of sorts that told of her unhappiness, her realization that I could never love her as she needed to be loved. That's what she wrote: "I realize now Luc can never love me as I want to be loved".' He said each word as if it were a jagged shard hurting his throat, his memory. He shook his head, closing his eyes briefly. 'And more, so much more, about how unhappy she was. She hated her life and she wrote about how she wanted to escape it—escape it *for ever*—just two weeks before she died.'

'I'm sorry,' Abby whispered, knowing the words were inadequate.

'I left the chateau and drove straight to Paris. I was numb, shocked—I'd had no idea she felt that way. No idea it was my fault. I thought it was just the miscarriage, you see. I'd *absolved* myself.'

Abby felt tears sting her eyes, gather behind her lids. She blinked them away. 'But it *wasn't* your fault, Luc—'

He spoke over her, refusing to listen, to hear. 'I had the chateau closed up that day. I didn't want to live here, I couldn't, not when I knew what a misery it had been for another person, what my ambition had cost. I haven't been back since…until today.' He stopped in front of her, raising one hand as if to touch her, caress her, but he didn't. He let his hand fall back to his side. 'I went to your concert that night because I needed to get out of my own head. My own thoughts. And then when I saw you…' He shook his head. 'I felt hope. More than I'd ever thought to. I felt myself coming alive just looking at you, speaking with you. And when we were together…'

He stopped, swallowing, and Abby felt again the rush of tears, of emotion. 'But I couldn't stay. I couldn't drag you into my problems, my pain. I couldn't. So I left. I know it seemed like a selfish act, but it wasn't meant to be one.' He paused, his gaze fastened on her, his eyes steady, yet also pleading for understanding. For absolution. 'And I'm so sorry for the hurt it caused you.'

Abby nodded, accepting Luc's apology, granting him atonement. Her mind whirled with Luc's revelations. 'And now?' she finally managed, holding her breath, waiting, *hoping* for Luc's answer…

He took a long time—too long—to reply. 'I don't know,' he finally said. 'I thought I'd never marry again. I didn't think I was capable of loving anyone the way they needed to be loved. I failed Suzanne in so many ways.' He shook his head. 'I don't want to fail anyone like that again.'

'Then what?' Abby asked, her voice hoarse with suppressed longing and fear. 'You're going to close yourself off from everything, everyone, for the rest of your life? Never take a chance again?'

'I didn't think it was even a possibility,' Luc confessed. 'I've been so numb, so blank all the time. Like there was nothing inside me. And then I met you.' He drew in a deep, shuddering breath and reached out to skim the tips of his fingers across her cheek. Abby closed her eyes. 'And I felt. I felt so much, wonderful, terrifying, and I'm not sure of anything any more.'

'I am.' It was so easy, surprisingly easy, to open her eyes, to smile at him as she reached out and drew him slowly to her, their bodies colliding, her bump between them. Her fingers tangled in his hair, drawing his face towards her so their lips brushed in the barest of kisses.

She felt Luc's hesitation, felt them both teeter on the precipice, knew he wanted to kiss her and yet felt he should pull back. But she wouldn't let him. She deepened the kiss, drawing him to her even more, so she fell back against the piano, her backside landing on the keys, creating a wonderful, dissonant melody.

Luc's resistance melted away and he responded to the kiss, deepening it so their tongues met and met again; Abby felt as if they were communicating, pouring their souls and hearts into one another. It was an endless kiss, a kiss made all the more sweet by the knowledge that there was no more they could do now. This kiss was it, everything, healing, hope and joy all poured into one as their bodies picked out a new melody on the piano and the sunlight streamed in, golden, mellow and pure.

CHAPTER TWELVE

THINGS changed after that. The farmhouse lost its atmosphere of silent tension, and the spring days slid towards summer, warm and golden.

They didn't talk about the future, and Abby made herself not care. Surely this was enough, this time together, eating, laughing, loving? Surely this was love? Luc had never said the words. Yet Abby felt it, felt something good had happened that day at the chateau, even though they remained at the farmhouse and the chateau stayed draped in dust sheets, a new lock on the iron gates.

Surely it was all only a matter of time?

She spent the days learning to cook, scouring the nearby markets with Luc for bunches of basil and fat cloves of garlic, glass bottles of cloudy olive-oil and balsamic vinegar. She loved the sensual nature of food: the fuzzy skin of a peach, the earthy smell of a potato. Not all of her experiments in the kitchen were a success, but Luc gamely tried them all anyway.

As the evenings grew warmer they ate out on the little terrace at the back, Chateau Mirabeau no more than two dark towers on the horizon amidst the trees. Yet the estate, and all of its implications, was ever-present in Abby's mind, for she wondered how Luc could move on as long as it remained shuttered and empty. Begin again, with her. The shadows and ghosts of the past had been banished, but they were not gone completely. They lurked in the dark corners of Abby's mind, tormented her at night as she lay alone, aching for Luc's touch, for his body next to hers, warm and solid.

Although they now spent every evening together, eating and talking, sharing all the things Abby had wanted to know and tell, Luc was still distant. The brush of his cool lips against her skin made her ache and yearn for more. She wanted to grab him by the lapels, drag him into her room and kiss him senseless. Yet even now she feared rejection. He might not physically leave her here, she acknowledged, but emotionally he was certainly capable of vacating the premises. Their emotional connection was fragile and tenuous, and Abby was not yet ready to test its new strength.

One afternoon Luc took her for a walk along the hills behind the farmhouse.

'Just where are we going?' Abby asked, tilting her head to the sun that poured over them like a benediction.

'You'll see.' Luc reached for the bag slung over his shoulder.

'What are you doing?'

He fumbled in the bag and then withdrew what looked like some sticks and fabric. It took Abby a second to realize what it was—a kite. 'It's a perfect day for flying a kite,' he said, and grinned. Abby had never seen him smile quite so much before. It lightened his countenance, brightened his already very blue eyes and softened the hard, chiselled planes of his cheeks and jaw. It made the breath catch in her throat and thoughts fly clean out of her head.

'A kite,' she repeated slowly, and in her mind's eye she could see herself sitting in the bar at Hotel Le Bristol across from Luc, her feet tucked up under her, starry-eyed, on her way to being seduced.

If you could do anything...what would it be?

She watched now as Luc assembled the kite, hooking the flimsy fabric over the wooden sticks, a diamond of bright-green nylon. She felt a ball of emotion lodge in her throat at the thought that Luc had remembered, that he wanted to give this to her.

'Shall we?' Luc gestured to the kite already flapping restlessly in the wind.

'All right.'

Luc took the kite's spool and began to unwind the string. He tossed the kite away from him, up into the sky, and Abby couldn't keep a bubble of laughter rising from within her as the kite caught the wind and began to rise. 'Oh, look!' she cried, clapping her hands, as giddy as a child.

Luc began to run backwards, unwinding more string as the kite started to soar. Abby tilted her head back, amazed at the simple yet glorious sight of the bright-green diamond bobbing among the clouds, high and free.

'You want to try?' Luc called to her after they'd watched the kite zigzag high above them for a few minutes. He'd moved several-hundred feet away in his attempt to keep the kite high in the sky.

'I couldn't,' Abby protested, even though she knew she was itching to take the spool in her hands. 'I've never—'

'I know.' Luc grinned again. 'Now's your chance.'

Laughing again—she couldn't help it—Abby jogged over to where he was. 'What should I…'

'Just take it.' Luc handed her the spool, and the string unwound a few more feet before Abby could stop it.

'Oh, no!'

'Walk backwards.'

Carefully she moved backwards amid the long grass, keeping the string taut by instinct as well as memory; she'd watched those happy children on the Heath many times.

'Good. See? You're doing it.'

'I am,' she called back, elated, triumphant, and she laughed aloud, the wind whipping around her, blowing her hair from its ponytail. At that moment the whole world suddenly seemed wide open, all things possible, everything free and light. Then the kite dipped. Abby's fingers tightened reflexively around the spool of string. 'Oh no!'

'Here.' Luc stood behind her, his arms reaching around to take in the slack string. The kite weaved and bobbed for a few seconds before it straightened, soaring once more. Luc remained behind Abby, his hands over hers as together they held the string and made the kite fly again.

Abby was achingly conscious of his hard chest behind her; another inch and she could lean her head against him, as she knew she wanted to. She worked to rest in his embrace now and for ever.

'Careful,' Luc murmured in her ear, and Abby realized the kite had started to dip once more. He pulled the string taut to save the swooping kite, but they'd left it too late, and in a long, graceful arc the kite plunged to earth. Abby stepped away from Luc and the shelter of his body.

'I think that's the end of the kite,' she said, moving closer to inspect the ripped fabric and snapped sticks.

'So it would seem,' Luc returned wryly. He folded up the wrecked kite and slipped it back into his bag. 'Still, it was worth it, don't you think?'

Was it? Abby wondered. Was any of this worth it? Things had changed since that afternoon in the chateau; things were wonderful, in a way. But were they real? They'd never talked about the future. They'd never told each other how they felt. Love was a word that hadn't been spoken. Whatever they had now, was it worth it, if it was all they were ever going to have?

Luc's eyes met hers, as blue, as intense and knowing as ever. The moment stretched and spiralled between them as the wind whipped around them, tangling Abby's hair and making her shove her hands deeper into the pockets of her jeans.

'We should go back,' he said after a moment, and Abby nodded. She was glad they'd flown the kite, but she knew neither of them had expected this uneasy tension to stretch between them, filled with all the things neither of them seemed ready to face or say.

A month had gone by since that day in the chateau when Luc told her over breakfast, 'We go to Paris in two days. You have a scan booked to check your condition.'

Abby crumbled a piece of roll onto her plate. 'Shall we take the train?'

'Jet,' Luc replied succinctly, reminding her just who and what he was. He paused. 'Perhaps we should make a weekend of it.' His voice was light, yet Abby tensed anyway. 'You need some new maternity clothes, don't you? We can go shopping.'

Abby made a face. 'For maternity clothes?'

'*Bien sûr.* Even pregnant women can be fashionable these days, can't they?'

'I suppose…' Her fashionable days were long behind her, along with piano, concerts and that jet-setting lifestyle. Yet the prospect of new clothes was, she'd realized, a little bit enticing. Even more so was the thought of being in Paris with him again. They'd be back where it had all started—yet would things be different this time?

It was a perfect, cloudless afternoon as they landed in Paris, the air warm and redolent of summer, even though it had just turned April.

They took a hired car to the private consultant Luc had booked, and soon Abby was lying on an examining-table, the cold, clear jelly squeezed onto her noticeably bigger bump as the consultant took the electric wand and began the scan.

The image of her baby squirming and filling the screen brought a smile to both her and Luc's faces.

'Quite an active little one you have in there,' the consultant said with a smile. 'And it looks as if your placenta previa has cleared considerably. Let me get a closer look…' He prodded Abby's bump a bit more, and she held her breath, hoping, praying for good news.

'Yes, it's completely gone,' he confirmed. 'Congratulations. All normal activities can be resumed.' He gave Luc a humorous glance. 'Which I'm sure you're happy about.'

Luc didn't reply, but Abby felt awareness fizz through every nerve of her body. Sex. The consultant was talking about sex. Now there was no reason for Luc to stay away at night, no reason for them not to consummate their relationship once more.

What relationship? an inner voice mocked. *You're only in France, only with Luc, because of the baby. He's never said any different, and you're too scared to ask him. Some relationship!*

She tried to silence that sly, mocking whisper, but it continued anyway. *You're afraid he'll reject you…again. Afraid he'll creep away, close himself off…again.*

She closed her eyes and felt Luc's hand on her arm, warm and reassuring. 'Abby? Is everything all right?'

'Yes.' She opened her eyes and glanced up at Luc; his own eyes were shadowed with concern. She smiled. 'I'm just so relieved.'

'As am I. This is good news indeed.'

After leaving the consultant's they had lunch at an elegant, expensive bistro before heading to the Champs Elysées for the promised shopping. Abby hadn't expected to enjoy shopping for maternity clothes, and she hadn't reckoned on Luc finding the sort of luxury boutique she didn't even know existed.

From the moment she entered the store she was pampered,

seated on a plush, suede sofa while models paraded the latest maternity styles: beautiful wrap-dresses and flowing tunic-tops, comfy trousers and skirts, and not a bow or bobble in sight.

She tried on a few of the outfits herself, liking the way the material flowed over her bump. It made her feel surprisingly confident, sensual, in a way she hadn't expected.

'They're gorgeous,' Abby admitted, and Luc smiled.

'They'll look gorgeous on you.' With a flick of his wrist, he indicated the growing pile of clothes that Abby had tried on. 'We'll take them all.'

'All! I don't need—'

'This isn't about need,' Luc told her as the assistant began to box the clothes up. 'It's about want.' He gave her a wolfish smile that made Abby's insides curl up, her stomach diving in a way that was altogether too pleasant. 'What I want. Now.' He glanced at his watch. 'I'll arrange for these to be sent to our hotel. You have another appointment upstairs.'

'I do?'

An assistant materialized by her elbow. 'Miss Summers, if you'll come with me?' Curious as well as a little nervous, Abby followed the svelte young woman upstairs to a maternity spa. 'Monsieur le Comte has booked an afternoon of treatments for you,' the assistant told her. 'Starting with a full-body massage.'

'A full-body massage?' Abby repeated, and felt herself begin to relax already.

For the next few hours Abby was plied with lotions, oils and aromatherapies, pummelled and pampered, so that when she finally left the spa she practically floated on air, drowsy and relaxed from all the treatments.

Luc was waiting for her in the lobby. He smiled when he saw her, a genuine smile that lit his eyes and softened his features; Abby found herself grinning back.

'You look relaxed.'

'So relaxed I could fall asleep,' Abby admitted.

'Don't fall asleep just yet. I have dinner reservations at Le Cinq.'

'You do?' Abby felt a new tingle spread over her that had little to do with the massage and therapies she'd received and everything to do with the way Luc smiled, his eyes glinting, turning them a deep azure.

'Of course. And your clothes have been delivered to our suite, so you can wear something new if you like.'

Abby's mind buzzed with these revelations as Luc ushered her into their private-hire car, a luxury sedan with tinted windows and plush leather seats.

Within minutes they'd navigated through Parisian traffic, cars facing a dozen different directions around L'Arc de Triomphe, before the sedan sleekly pulled up to the front arches of the George V hotel. A bellboy opened the door and Abby practically floated into the marble foyer, Luc by her side.

Luc had booked the royal suite, and as Abby stepped into the luxurious living-room, with its gilt tables and marble floor, ornate paintings and antiques filling every inch of the exquisite space, she was reminded with sudden, stinging force of the last time she'd been in a hotel such as this. A hotel just a mile or two away. Her heart had been beating in her throat; she'd been as young, hopeful and naïve as any girl could be.

She was different now, older, wiser, more confident. Yet also more afraid for, just as before, she didn't know what would happen tonight, what *could* happen.

As she turned to Luc who stood in the doorway with a smile flickering across his mouth and lurking in his eyes, she felt a new, heady hope that this night could be different. That this night could repair the first night, heal and fulfil it. It could be the happy ending, she thought almost incredulously, to the fairy tale.

If Luc would allow it.

He walked towards her, smiling openly now. 'You look surprised to be here.' He stopped in front of her, his hands coming up to slide down her shoulders, holding her in a half-embrace.

'I am,' Abby admitted. 'Surprised and happy. It's been a wonderful day.'

'Good.' Luc leaned down and slowly, achingly, brushed his lips with hers. Abby closed her eyes as she leaned into the kiss and gave herself to it fully, as if with that simple, little kiss she could communicate all she felt to Luc, all she hoped and wanted, and even needed.

The kiss ended all too soon, and Luc pulled away before leaning his forehead against hers. They remained that way for a moment, still, silent, waiting. Abby didn't want to break the fragile moment by speaking, yet words were needed.

'Luc, what's wrong?' she asked quietly. He closed his eyes, his face so close she could feel the whispery brush of his lashes against her skin.

'I don't want this to end,' he whispered.

'It doesn't have to,' Abby said simply. Her heart felt light, lighter than air, with relief. Was that all that was worrying Luc?

'No,' he said slowly, his hands coming up to cup her face as he absorbed this seemingly new revelation. 'It doesn't have to.'

Several hours later, after a nap, Abby stood in the dressing room of the royal suite, smoothing the silky, silver-grey material of her gown over her hips. She looked and felt beautiful, lush, sensuous. The gown fell from a halter top, the material draping over her bump and emphasizing its womanly curve. She left her hair loose, falling in soft waves over her shoulders. Smiling a little, she reached for the matching filmy wrap and headed out to the living room.

Luc stood in the centre of the room, devastating in a finely cut suit of lightweight wool that emphasized his broad shoulders and trim hips, his eyes blazingly blue as he turned to smile at her, his gaze sweeping over her form.

'You look amazing.' The sentiment was so heartfelt and sincere that Abby could do nothing but respond in the same manner.

'So do you.'

They gazed at each other for a moment, smiling, until with a little laugh Abby admitted, 'And I'm starving.' She patted her bump. 'This little one needs food.'

'And, what madam wants, madam shall have,' Luc replied with a short bow, and he moved to put an arm around her shoulders, drawing her close to the warm shelter of his body as he led her out of the suite and downstairs to the hotel's Michelin-starred restaurant, Le Cinq.

It didn't seem fair to be this happy, Abby thought as they entered the restaurant with its thick Turkish carpet and glinting chandeliers. A tuxedoed waiter bowed and showed them to a private table in the back.

Abby slid into the seat and took the menu from the waiter; its script was an elegant cursive. 'Did you order already?' she asked Luc, and he shook his head.

'Not this time.'

Abby smiled, a new satisfaction blooming within her, for surely she was not the only one to have changed? It was a small thing, she acknowledged, yet still important. She glanced down at the menu, scanning the various decadent offerings.

In the end they feasted on salmon caviar and black truffles, a delicate saddle of lamb and fresh, tender asparagus. Yet Abby barely noticed the food she put in her mouth, hungry as she was. She was too aware, totally aware, of Luc, of his eyes so very warm on hers, of his smile, no more than a brief curl of his wonderfully mobile mouth, still managing to light Abby's insides with both joy and hope.

After dessert they rose as one from the table. The restaurant was now nearly empty, only a few couples lingering among the candlelit tables, as they had been. Abby could already feel a heavy, heady expectancy start to build within her as Luc laced her fingers with his own and led her to the elevator.

They didn't speak, just as they hadn't before that night over a year ago when Abby's life had changed for the first time. Now she felt as if it might change again, and she welcomed it, wanted it, more than she'd wanted anything before.

They stepped into the suite. The lamps were turned down and a basket of fresh fruit and chocolates, provided by the maid service, awaited them in the lounge.

'I should change,' she said, and heard the wobble of nervousness in her voice. Luc turned to her and smiled.

'But you look so beautiful. Is the dress comfortable?'

'Yes,' Abby admitted. 'But my feet hurt.'

'That's easily remedied.' Luc gestured for her to sit down, and when she did he ran his fingers along her calves, sending what felt like a shower of sparks racing through her body. Then he slipped off the high-heeled sandals she'd been wearing. His long, strong fingers massaged her feet, finding the sensitive and aching places without her even saying a word; Abby leaned her head back against the sofa, almost groaning with relaxed comfort.

'That feels really good,' she murmured, and let herself lie passive at Luc's wonderful ministrations. Yet as relaxing as it was, she also felt the energy of awareness fire through her; when Luc's hands slid from her feet up her legs, his palms gliding over the slippery material of her dress to rest on her hips, it felt like the most natural and right thing in the world. He knelt in front of her, his cheek pressed against her bump.

The baby kicked, and they both laughed. 'Ouch,' Luc said ruefully, rubbing his cheek. 'She's strong, isn't she?'

'She knows her own mind,' Abby agreed. She was so achingly conscious of Luc's hands on her hips, his body so close to hers, and she couldn't quite keep herself from reaching out and tangling her hands in the crisp softness of his hair, threading her fingers so she tilted his head up to face hers.

'Abby…' he breathed softly, her name both a question and a plea.

'Yes?' she replied, and it was all the answer he needed.

He leaned forward, his hands now sliding from her hips up to her shoulders, drawing her towards him so their lips met again and again; this time there was no hesitation, no question, no fear.

Luc pulled away after a long, wonderful moment. 'I don't want to hurt you,' he said. Abby didn't know whether he meant physically, because of the baby, or emotionally, because of their history. She gave the only answer she could.

'You won't.'

Then, with the moon slanting through the wide windows and washing the world in silver, he led her from the living room to the bedroom; the huge, king-sized bed-cover was already turned down by the maid, and the lamp spread a warm glow over the room.

He drew her to him again, kissing her with a soft passion that still told of his urgency, his need. Abby responded, shrugging out of her gown, which slithered to the floor in a whisper of silk. Luc unbuttoned his shirt, and when they were both naked he led her to the bed. Abby followed, unselfconscious, unafraid, finally believing in the truth, the reality, of this moment, and hoping it would last for ever.

* * *

Luc cradled Abby in his arms as her breathing slowed, and she drifted off to sleep. One hand rested possessively on her bump, and as the baby kicked under his hand he felt a thrill like a shiver race through him.

This won't last. It can't.

He wanted to banish that sly voice of his conscience, of memories, fears, sliding to the surface of his mind even as he tried to exorcise them. He'd never expected to experience this kind of love, deep, abiding, so much so that it was a part of him, all of him. He couldn't imagine life without it. Without Abby.

Yet what if he had to? What if he let Abby down again, just as he'd failed Suzanne? What if this happiness, this love, was nothing more than a mirage, a magical night just as their other nights together had been, not actually real?

Not real enough to last.

His hold tightened instinctively on Abby and she stirred in her sleep. He made himself relax, forced his mind to blank. He couldn't think about all the possibilities, the fear of things that could happen.

Maybe they wouldn't. Maybe they could have this moment for ever, could wake up again and again, morning after morning, to share another day together.

Maybe, this time, it would last. Nothing would go wrong, nothing would shatter the pure perfection of their love.

Abby woke up to sunlight streaming through the windows and the sound of a maid knocking on the door. She tensed, her gaze sliding to the clock by the bed. It was nearly noon.

She pulled the sheet up to her breasts as she glanced around the room, a plunging sensation deep in her middle as she took in the empty half of the bed, the clothes still scattered on the floor.

Where was Luc?

'Bonjour?' The maid called from the living room. Abby

closed her eyes. She felt as if she were reliving one of the worst moments of her life.

'*Bonjour,*' she heard a voice call back, and then a few seconds of conversation before the maid bid her farewell and the door of the suite clicked shut.

Luc came into the bedroom, his hair still damp from the shower, his shirt only halfway buttoned. He looked amazing, Abby thought. He stopped in the doorway, smiling, and as Abby's own smile widened into a great, big, sloppy grin, she felt her heart turn over—and knew this was the beginning of for ever.

CHAPTER THIRTEEN

'FOR EVER' lasted two months. Two wonderful, sun-soaked months, when they rarely ventured from the farmhouse, spending their days reading, relaxing, cooking and making love. Abby's skin took on a sun-kissed, peachy glow, and her bump grew hard and round.

Some evenings they lay in bed—having shared Luc's since they'd returned from Paris—and felt the baby roll and kick. They talked about names—Charlotte or Emilie—and wondered whose eyes she'd have. That was as close as they came to talking about any future together, and Abby told herself not to mind. Not to feel afraid.

There was time; there was surely lots of time for Luc to trust in this, in them. Abby didn't know exactly what was holding Luc back, but she felt it in the moment after they made love when he turned his body slightly away from her, even though his arm was still around her. She felt it in the sudden lapses into silence in a conversation when she'd see a shadow steal across Luc's face and settle in his eyes, and she'd know he was thinking. Remembering.

She wanted to ask him what he was afraid of, longed to press for answers, for declarations that she knew instinctively he wasn't ready to give or make. Yet sometimes, as they sat in the drowsy sunshine of late afternoon, the remnants of a delicious meal before them, she had to bite her lips to keep from crying out, *Why don't you tell me you love me? Why don't you talk about the future?*

She didn't, because she was afraid they might not have one. She argued silently with herself that after months with Luc she had no need to be afraid. Surely the days and nights they'd spent together, week after week, spoke of a deep and abiding love? Surely she should just gather her courage and confront him, ask him what he intended to do when the baby was born? What he wanted? Or perhaps she should simply tell him what she wanted. She wanted to stay in France, to live at the farmhouse, to have everything stay exactly as it was.

Yet even as this desire nestled in her soul Abby knew it wasn't possible. Perhaps it wasn't even right.

Nothing stayed the same. Things always changed.

'I'm going to Paris,' Luc told her one morning as she buttered her second croissant—her appetite had certainly increased—and she stilled, the knife in her hand. Did she imagine that slight sharpness to his tone?

'Oh? Do you have business there?' she asked eventually, for Luc had gone back to his newspaper as if the conversation was concluded, if there had ever really been one.

'Yes.' He looked up briefly, distracted, his smile no more than lip service. 'I'll only be gone the day. And you have my mobile number.'

'Yes.' Carefully Abby returned the knife to her plate. Her appetite had vanished. Luc wasn't asking her to accompany him to Paris, and she couldn't quite make herself ask to go. She didn't want to beg, didn't want to be rebuffed. Besides, she told herself, knowing it was at least partially a lie, she didn't really want to go to Paris. She was nearly eight months' pregnant, and she felt heavy, achy and tired. She would be fine here for the day; she'd nap, then cook something marvellous for dinner and not worry at all.

It didn't quite happen that way, of course. Abby stood at the window and watched Luc drive down the gravel lane, felt the emptiness of the house echo around her, before she turned away and wandered restlessly through the sun-dappled rooms.

This was ridiculous. She had plenty to do; she could read, or cook, or tidy, if she really felt like it. She could write a letter to her mother, who wanted to visit when the baby was born, or read her father's latest letter, which had come with a thick packet of positive reviews of his concert tour.

She decided instead to go for a walk. The sun was high above, shining brightly on the main road to Pont-Saint-Esprit, causing the pavement to glitter, and giving everything a hard, shiny edge. Abby might have deceived herself that she was simply going for a stroll, but she knew as soon as her pace began to slow she'd really only had one destination in mind.

Chateau Mirabeau.

She stopped in front of the gates; the padlock was made of bright, new steel. She touched it briefly; in the shadow of the rhododendrons flanking the gate it was cool to her touch. The gates were locked and the chateau was inaccessible once more. She knew that, had known it every time they'd driven past the chateau on a shopping trip to Pont-Saint-Esprit, when she'd glimpsed the locked gates from the car. Luc had never said a word about it, and neither had she.

Coward.

She shook her head slowly, ashamed and irritated with herself and her own fearful weakness. If she had any kind of relationship with Luc, any love or trust at all, surely she should be able to mention these things?

'Just a few little facts, like whether you're going to actually stick around,' she said aloud, her voice sharp. She realized she hadn't talked aloud to herself since Paris. She hadn't needed to; she'd always had Luc.

Yet now, the sun beating on her head, her fingers still

touching the padlock, she felt like she didn't have him. Maybe she'd never had him, not really. Not the way she wanted to, craved to—totally, unreservedly, without fear or worry.

No, she didn't have that. The very fact that she was here, gazing into the closed-up grounds of the chateau like some pathetic orphan from a fairy tale—a sad one—showed just how much was actually lacking in her relationship with Luc. She should be with him in Paris, or, if not, she should be comfortable and secure in the fact that he was there and she was not.

Instead fear bit at her, gnawed at her hope, and the sense of complacency which had cocooned her in a smug bubble these last two months.

Now the bubble had burst, and over something so small! Yet sometimes, Abby acknowledged starkly, the small things revealed larger things, things she'd been closing her eyes to, because the last few months had been so happy, so perfect.

So shallow.

The thought hurt, yet Abby felt it must be true if she could torture herself with such doubt now. Slowly, disconsolately, she turned away from the locked gates and all they signified.

The sound of a car approaching and the sudden spurt of gravel as its driver braked made Abby stop and whirl around, a ridiculous hope blooming inside her that perhaps Luc had returned, that he hadn't gone without her.

The hope soon died as an elegantly coiffed woman in her fifties exited the car and strode towards Abby with a look of almost desperate intent on her face. Abby froze, suddenly nervous. What if Luc had sold the chateau? Perhaps this woman owned it now and wanted Abby off her property. Her hands went instinctively, protectively, to her bump, cradling the life hidden inside.

'Do you live here?' the woman asked in French, her voice raw and harsh.

Abby shook her head, answering also in French. 'No. I was just looking.'

The woman's whole body seemed to sag for only a second, then she straightened and shook her head slowly. 'I had hoped…' she murmured, half to herself.

Abby's curiosity was piqued enough to repeat, 'Hoped?'

Her gaze snapped back to Abby, dropping to take in her obvious pregnancy. 'Do you know Comte de Gévaudan?' she asked, and Abby stiffened in surprise at Luc's formal title. Her hands tightened around her bump as she nodded.

'Yes.'

'You have not married him,' the woman concluded, still half-talking to herself, 'or it would have been in the newspapers. I would have heard.'

There was something almost possessive about the way she spoke, with her eyes narrowing, her head tilted to one side, that made Abby prickle uneasily. The woman did not speak out of malice, but there had to be some history here. 'You know him?' she asked, and the woman gave a short, unhappy laugh.

'Oh, yes. I know him. *Knew* him. Although we have not seen each other in nearly two years—since my daughter's funeral.' She spoke flatly, without emotion, and yet somehow it still conveyed an ocean of grief too wide and deep to cross with mere words. Abby knew who this woman must be.

'You're Suzanne's mother,' she said softly.

'Mireille Roget,' the woman confirmed. 'He told you about Suzanne? He spoke of her?'

'Yes, of course. He…' Abby struggled to convey what Luc had said, what he felt, yet how could she? She didn't even really know. 'He regrets Suzanne's death very much,' she finally said.

'I know he does,' Mireille replied. '*Mon Dieu*, the whole country knows! He lashed himself over it times enough. Shutting up the chateau, leaving the region…' She pointed at the shiny new lock on the gates. 'When I saw you there, I thought perhaps he'd opened it again, that he was living again.'

'You did?' Abby couldn't keep the surprise from her voice.

Mireille nodded. 'Losing my daughter was bad enough, *mademoiselle*. But to see another life wasted so pointlessly only adds to my grief. I know Luc blamed himself for Suzanne's unhappiness, and perhaps even for her death, but it was not his fault.'

'He doesn't see that,' Abby confessed quietly. 'He still feels guilty.'

'I had hope…' Mireille shook her head. 'But he is with you, yes? He is moving on, perhaps?'

'Perhaps,' Abby allowed, and heard how shaky her voice sounded. She felt suddenly, tremulously, on the verge of tears, and Mireille saw.

'This is no place for a conversation. Come, let me take you to Pont-Saint-Esprit. I was going there anyway, and we can have coffee. Talk. I think perhaps it will be good for both of us.'

Even though this woman was a stranger, Abby trusted her kindly, faded blue eyes, and let her lead her to the waiting car.

Once settled in a café with a large latte, Abby listened while Mireille spoke. Finally, she thought, she was hearing the other side of the story. She'd been afraid there hadn't even been one, and it was good to hear what Mireille had to say.

'Suzanne adored Luc—worshipped him, really—as the big brother she'd never had.' Mireille sighed, her hands cradling her cup of coffee. 'It was not, as I am sure you can imagine, the best basis for a marriage.'

'No,' Abby agreed, thinking that once she had felt the same way about Luc. Had idolised him, made him the shining knight in her fairy tale. But life wasn't a fairy tale, and Luc wasn't a knight. He was simply the man she loved.

'He was fond of her,' Mireille continued. 'And attentive, but it was never enough for Suzanne.' She sighed. 'Nothing would ever be enough.'

Abby swallowed, thinking of Luc's own similar words. *I could never love her as she'd needed to be loved.* And it was true, he hadn't been able to. Yet surely that was not his fault?

'She was always a melancholy child, and I suppose it worsened after her marriage.' Mireille pressed her lips together. 'I loved her so very much, and it still tears at me to know how unhappy she was. At least at the end…' She stopped, shaking her head, and took a sip of coffee to compose herself.

'At the end?' Abby prompted softly, and Mireille looked up, her eyes bright.

'She'd decided to divorce Luc. I never told him, because I knew he would blame himself for the failure of the marriage, but in reality it was a marriage that never should have happened. Suzanne was finally starting to realize that.' Mireille's hands tightened around her cup.

'The day she died, she was coming to visit me. She'd rung me, telling me she'd decided to finally move on with her life. She'd booked a course in Paris—teacher training. It was what she'd always wanted to do, but as chatelaine of Chateau Mirabeau she never felt she could.' Mireille shrugged. 'Who knows if that is the truth? Suzanne was afraid to tell Luc anything. She even hid from him the fact that she'd been so depressed and unhappy. The poor man only knew after her death.'

'She was coming to visit you?' Abby repeated, needing the clarification. Craving it. 'She was happy?'

'Yes. For the first time in years, perhaps. It comforts me, to know that.'

Abby swallowed, her heart starting to pound, her mouth dry. 'Luc wondered if—if Suzanne actually meant…'

It took Mireille a moment to understand what Abby couldn't quite bring herself to say. 'You mean to take her own life on the road? No, no. She would not—' She stopped, swallowed, and shook her head vigorously. 'She would not. She'd finally got her life on the right track. She was not about to go off it on purpose.'

'I'm glad,' Abby said, her voice heartfelt. 'For her sake…as well as for Luc's.'

'No wonder he tortures himself so.' Mireille shook her head. 'The accident report suggested that perhaps something had darted across the road and Suzanne had swerved to avoid it.' She smiled in bittersweet memory. 'She was always ridiculously fond of little animals. Me, I say put them in the cooking pot!'

'Mireille, thank you for speaking with me.' Abby covered the older woman's hand with her own. 'I hope—I pray—it will make some difference.'

'With Luc?' She gestured to Abby's bump. 'His?'

Abby blushed. 'Yes,' she admitted, although there was no need to confirm it. The answer was obvious.

'You love him?' Mireille asked after a moment.

'Yes,' she whispered.

'Then I will pray for you. He needs to move on. To love someone properly, and let himself be loved. What he had with Suzanne…' Mireille shook her head. 'It was not right. But perhaps with you…' She squeezed Abby's hand. 'I will pray.'

Abby nodded, her heart too full to speak. The hope Mireille had offered, in both revealing Luc's past and addressing his future, made her feel weak and dizzy with relief.

The feeling continued as they left the café and Mireille drove her back to the farmhouse. Abby was tired enough to lie her head back against the seat and close her eyes, and she wondered if she'd actually dozed off when Mireille gently touched her shoulder.

'Abigail…we are here.'

'What?' Abby blinked, disoriented, the dizzy feeling still present and growing stronger. She struggled to sit up and open the door of the car, but it felt as if there were a veil across her eyes, muting Mireille's voice and dimming the world.

'Abigail, *ça va?*' Real concern sharpened Mireille's voice.

'I'm fine…' Then Abby looked down and registered the dark blood staining her jeans, the seat of the car. It seemed to be everywhere; how could there be so *much?* Then the veil drew even more firmly closed, and she slumped forward, unconscious.

The tinny trill of Luc's mobile cut through the still air of the conference room in Paris. A sheaf of documents lay spread across the table, detailing the sale of Chateau Mirabeau. Luc stilled, pen in hand.

'Pardonnez-moi.'

He flipped open his mobile and spoke tersely into it. 'Luc Toussaint. *Oui?*'

'Luc. It's Mireille.' He tensed at the sound of the older woman's voice, shock and a growing sense of dread spreading through him. He hadn't spoken to Mireille in months. There had been grief and fear in those three little words, and it brought back the last time she'd rung, when she'd also told him, 'There's been an accident.'

For a moment he couldn't actually credit that she'd said it, the same words as before, nearly two years ago, when he'd sat in a similar conference room, the phone pressed to his ear as his world had dissolved into numbness, nothingness.

It was happening again.

'Abby.' The word was forced out through his throat, which had shut, as his whole body seemed to have, every nerve and fibre shutting down as he struggled to retain focus. Composure. 'Why are— *How* can you be calling about Abby?'

'We met this morning. We spoke.'

'No.' He closed his eyes, choked on a sob. He couldn't bear to hear it, to have his world fall apart again—and so much worse this time, so much *more*. *'No.'*

'Luc, no! It's not that. She's alive. But the baby—she's been taken to hospital.'

Grim resolve replaced the agonizing fear, and once again he clamped down on the emotion. 'I'll be there in two hours.'

'I'm sorry,' Mireille choked, but Luc had already snapped his phone shut. He rose from the table, tossing the pen aside.

'Monsieur Le Comte?'

He blinked, bringing the room—and what he'd been about to do—into focus, realizing with sudden, sharp clarity how misguided he'd been. How stupid. *'Pardonnez-moi,'* he murmured, and strode out, the business deal completely forgotten. All he could think about, hope for, was Abby.

Abby. The woman he loved. The woman he couldn't lose.

She woke slowly, blinking the hospital room into view, everything still feeling muted and surreal. Unnatural. Her hands flew to her bump and she gasped aloud, a cry of shock and fear—for, where once there had been a hard, round baby squirming and kicking her way to life, now there was nothing. Nothing but the soft, pillowy flesh of an empty womb.

'My baby…' Her words came out in a desperate croak, and she heard someone stir next to her before Luc's face came into view. His hand reached for hers, gently squeezing strength and warmth into them.

'She's all right, Abby. She's safe.'

'Where…?'

'You had an emergency C-section. Your placenta had detached—it's called a placenta abruption—and you were in grave danger. Fortunately, Mireille realized that, and took you directly to Accident and Emergency in Pont-Saint-Esprit. They operated immediately, and our daughter is fine. Small, but fine.' Luc spoke steadily, but even in her state Abby could hear the ragged edge of emotion underneath.

'You came back.'

'Mireille called me on my mobile. I never should have left.' The ragged edge became more pronounced, fraying his tone and composure. 'I thought for *one* day.' He shook his head. 'Thank God you're safe. You're both safe.'

Abby nodded, relief pouring through her. 'Can I see her?'

'She's in the special-care unit at the moment, simply because she was so early, but I'll have a nurse bring her to you as soon as possible.'

Abby nodded. She felt perilously close to tears, full of emotion, of delayed fear, hope and love. She turned to Luc, reaching again for his hand. His fingers closed over hers, strong and reassuring. 'I'm glad you're here.'

'I only wish I could have been here sooner. I never should have left you alone.'

'Who could have guessed this would happen, after the scan? You can't be with me always.'

'No.'

They both lapsed into silence, and Abby wished she could say more. Ask more. She desperately needed to know what Luc wanted now that the baby was born. She knew he would expect her to return to the farmhouse at least until she was recovered, but what then? The last thing she wanted to be was a liability, loving Luc more than he could love her back, to be unhappy, unsatisfied.

Just like Suzanne had been.

Better to get on with her life now, recover and heal both her body and heart…alone. 'Luc…' she started, her voice scratchy. She wasn't even sure what she dared to say.

'Shh.' Luc patted her hand. 'I should let you rest. They'll

bring the baby up soon.' He got up, smiling briefly, but even in her hazy state Abby saw how distracted he was, how distant, and her heart felt leaden within her. She turned her face away so he wouldn't see the tears glittering in her eyes, dampening her cheeks.

'All right.'

He didn't answer, and in the silence Abby knew he had gone.

CHAPTER FOURTEEN

LUC pulled the car to a stop in front of the gates, now washed in moonlight. He'd come directly from the hospital, from Abby's room, where she'd sat up in bed, cradling their little girl. They'd decided on Emilie Charlotte. She was as pink and delicate as a rosebud, everything about her, from her pouty lips to her little fists tightly and perfectly furled. His heart ached with the memory of that precious sight, and it wasn't an altogether pleasant feeling. It hurt more than he thought it would: the knowledge of how much he'd been given, and how much he still might stand to lose.

He sat in the car for a moment, listening to the wind rattle the padlock, the sound echoing and lonely. After a moment he finally got out of the car, the key heavy in his pocket.

It turned easily—it was new, after all—and soon he was walking down the familiar, sweeping lane, his shoes crunching on the gravel. Chateau Mirabeau was no more than a silhouette against the night sky, yet he knew its shape so well, so intimately, that he didn't even hesitate as he crossed the front lawn and made his way up the steps to the main entrance.

He let himself in quietly; the door creaking was the only sound. Once in the foyer he simply stood and breathed in the scent of the place, of dust, must and over a year of neglect, but with a faint hint of lavender-polish and *home*.

This was home.

He breathed in deeply, the night air still and sultry as he moved through the rooms. The last time he'd been here, when Abby had found her way in, he'd been in such a rush to find her he hadn't really taken note of his surroundings. Perhaps he'd blinded himself on purpose, unable to bear the sight of his beloved home shrouded in dust sheets—forgotten because he'd chosen to forget it, because remembering had been too painful.

The day he'd realized his attachment to this place, his obsession, and that all it meant might have cost a life—his wife's life—had been one of the worst he'd ever known. He'd felt guilt, shame, grief and pain all course through him in hot, unrelenting rivers, so deep, wide and all-consuming that he'd simply shut them off—shut himself off—and allowed himself to feel nothing at all.

He'd decided to be numb, blank, because feeling nothing was easier. It had been a choice, he saw now, even if it hadn't felt like it at the time. It had always been a choice, perhaps even back when his father had died so suddenly, leaving a gaping hole where a family had been. He'd decided to love the chateau rather than people because buildings didn't die. They didn't hurt you, and you couldn't disappoint them.

Except, he thought now as he looked at one of his favourite salons decked out in dust sheets—at the gilded woodwork his mother had loved so well, now chipped and peeling—perhaps you could disappoint buildings after all.

He was tired of disappointment, weary of guilt, exhausted by fear. He'd never, *never*, been so afraid as when Mireille had rung him to tell him Abby was in the hospital, that her life and their child's life was in danger. Luc shuddered even now in memory. He'd felt his whole life tilt and slide; everything he'd believed to be true had blown away like so much insubstantial ash.

He'd thought loving Abby would be hard, that the risk of hurting her, failing her, was too great. He'd shut himself off from the possibility of a future with her because of those risks. Yet in that moment, when he'd realized Abby might be lost to him so utterly, he'd realized the truth: losing her would be worse.

And now he was left with a choice. He could choose to return to safety, to his numb, emotionless state where he hurt nobody and nobody hurt him. He could keep the chateau as locked and lifeless as a tomb. Or he could sell it, as he'd been planning to that afternoon, thinking that the only way ahead was to pretend the past didn't exist.

Or he could take a risk. He could choose love rather than safety, life over numbness. He could choose to feel, even if feeling held its own pain with the rush of emotions, which were terrifying in their strength.

He needed to choose.

The house creaked and settled around him, the sound like a sigh. Slowly Luc reached out and touched a nearby sheet, clenching the cool cloth under his fingers. He pulled slowly at first, and then harder, until the sheet fell away completely—and the living began.

Abby moved slowly through the farmhouse, Emilie cradled in her arms. It was a week since her daughter's birth, and everything still felt new and fragile.

Uncertain.

She glanced down at her daughter's sleeping face, her lips pursed as though in concentration, and knew that at least one thing was certain. One thing—her daughter's life—was shining, pure, absolute.

'I'll put her in the cradle,' she told Luc, who hovered in the doorway, his expression both distracted and strained.

'I moved all her things to the study,' he told her. 'Since you're not meant to climb stairs.'

Abby made a wry face. 'What things?'

Luc smiled sheepishly. 'I ordered things from Paris. One of everything I could think of.'

Abby nodded and headed towards the study. She stopped in the doorway, amazed at the room's transformation. It was bedecked in white-and-pink tulle, with a huge cot, a dresser, a glider, and at least two-dozen different baby toys. 'You really went to town.'

'We should have bought things before.'

Abby nodded again. 'We weren't really prepared, were we?' They'd both been hiding from reality, from the future and all of its uncertainty. Yet now, drawing in a breath, she knew it needed to be faced. She laid Emilie in the huge cot, tucking the pretty white blankets around her. When she was sure the baby was settled, she turned back to Luc.

Time to face the truth. The future.

Luc stood in the doorway of the study-cum-nursery, a look of rapt wonder on his face as he watched Abby settle Emilie. It gave her a treacherous flicker of hope. Then she squared her shoulders and clung to her resolution. A single look was not enough.

'Luc…' she began, but he held a finger to his lips and shook his head.

'You'll wake Emilie.'

'Then let's go outside,' Abby said firmly, and led the way through the living room to the terrace. The air was dry and warm and fell over Abby like a comforting blanket. She'd miss this place, she thought with a pang of sorrow. She'd miss these months she and Luc had shared—but most of all she'd just miss Luc.

She'd miss the smile he gave her over the rim of his newspaper, the way his eyes glinted so knowingly, the way he held her, cradled in his arms like a treasure, after they'd made love. She'd miss it all. But mostly she'd miss what they hadn't yet shared—the possibility of living and loving together, of becoming closer and closer as they watched their daughter blossom and grow.

She swallowed, forcing the regrets away, and turned to Luc. 'I'll need to stay here for a few weeks to recover, but then I think I should go.' The words came out with far more determination than she felt; all she could feel was the ache of misery and loss like a molten lump in her chest.

For one glorious second Luc looked shocked, horrified, and hope leapt within Abby. Then his face blanked, any emotion wiped clean away, and he gave a little shrug that felt like a dagger to the heart, inserted and twisted.

'If that is what you want.'

What an indifferent little phrase, Abby thought with a spurt of anger. What a horrible *nothing* thing to say after all they'd shared. She'd just had his *child*. 'Is that all you can say?' she demanded in a raw voice, and Luc stiffened, surprise etched on his features.

'Isn't it what you want me to say?' he asked in a low voice.

'What I want?' Abby repeated, choking on the words. 'What *I want*?' Luc shrugged, his expression now taut, trapped, becoming remote. Abby sagged, her anger replaced by weary despair. 'What have we been doing these last few months, Luc—having a good time? Neither of us has ever mentioned the future, or what's going to happen. We've never…'

She took a breath and forced herself to continue. 'We've never even said what we feel for each other, if anything.' When Luc didn't even respond, the last little hope that he loved her and wanted her to stay flickered out to ash. She took another deep breath. 'We've both buried our heads in the sand, and we can't any more.' His expression, so blank and ominous, didn't change. '*I* can't,' she amended quietly. 'I want more. And I realize I'm not going to get it from you.'

Luc didn't speak, didn't blink, didn't do anything, and something in Abby needed a reaction. 'So?' she demanded harshly. 'Are you going to say anything—like goodbye, at least?'

'I should,' Luc replied after a long moment. 'I should let you go. I've been telling myself that for days, weeks—that you'd be better off without me.'

'Are you sure you don't mean *you'd* be better off without *me*?' Abby retorted sharply. 'I'm not going to let you hide behind your fear any longer, Luc. You've told me before that you walked away because you didn't want to hurt me. Well, that won't wash this time.' She threw her shoulders back, met his trapped gaze with her own glittering challenge. 'If you're going to walk away this time, then let's be honest about it. It's not because you're afraid of hurting me. It's because you're afraid of getting hurt *yourself*.'

'What—?' The single word was a hiss of disbelief and denial.

'Because love hurts, doesn't it? Feelings can hurt. Caring opens you up to pain, to the *possibility* of pain, which can be so utterly terrifying. You know, after you left that night and my career went to pieces, I felt numb. I know how comforting that can be. Sometimes it's necessary, for a time. It's part of grieving. But eventually you've got to rejoin the living. You've got to move on. You've got to choose. Choose life, choose love.' She paused then ploughed on. 'Choose me.'

Luc let out a long, ragged breath. 'I want to choose you,' he said in a voice so low Abby strained to hear. 'But…' He bowed his head, his shoulders hunched, one hand rising of its own accord to cover his face. 'I've been so *afraid*.'

'Oh, Luc—' Abby's voice broke along with her resolve, and she crossed to wrap her arms around him. He submitted to her embrace, his shoulder silently shaking. They stood that way for a long moment, neither of them speaking. Finally Luc drew in a shuddering breath and lifted his head, pressing his forehead to Abby's.

'The other night,' he began haltingly, 'after I first left you in hospital, I began to wonder if maybe all these things I'd been telling myself, all these things I believed… Maybe they weren't true after all. Just what you said, Abby. You know me so well.' She felt rather than saw him smile, and reached up to touch his cheek. 'I believed you'd be better off without me. I believed I'd disappoint or hurt you, and so I thought I was doing the right thing.' He pressed her fingers to his lips. 'Then I realized, when I went to Chateau Mirabeau—'

'You went to Chateau Mirabeau?' Abby whispered, not quite understanding why this gave her hope.

'Yes. I was going to sell it, you know, that day in Paris. I thought—I thought that might help me to forget everything that has gone before. But you can't run from your past, you can only try to heal it.' His hands slid up under the heavy mass of her hair to cup her face. 'Abby, I thought I was being noble. I thought I was protecting you. But you were right— I was really protecting myself.'

Abby waited, holding her breath, *hoping*. 'I've been afraid to feel…to love.' He drew in a breath, as if he were a drowning man gasping for air. 'Afraid of hurting you, but also of being hurt.' Abby knew how much it must be costing him to make such a confession, to be so vulnerable. Yet still he continued, finally needing to say it all.

'I acted selfishly, leaving you, telling you I couldn't give you what you needed. It was out of fear and self-preservation, not the altruistic motives I attributed to my actions.' He shook his head. 'The heart is ever-deceitful, I suppose.'

'But you're being honest now,' Abby whispered. 'Why?'

'Because when I saw you in the hospital, so pale, so *lifeless*—' Luc choked, and Abby saw a sheen of tears in his eyes. 'I realized I could lose you…really lose you. It terrified me, Abby.' He tried to smile and almost succeeded. 'All this time I've been telling myself I should let you go, and then, when it was actually a possibility and not by choice... I drove away from the hospital that first night in a near-trance of fear. I was running away, I suppose, because these feelings—feeling so much—scared me. I'd been numb, blessedly numb, for so long. And then I came to Chateau Mirabeau. I walked through the rooms and realized I couldn't sell it. I *shouldn't*. It's a part of me, and selling it wouldn't accomplish what I wanted it to. Only loving you could do that.'

'Luc, you know what Mireille told me—about the accident?'

'She told me too,' Luc said quietly. 'While you were in hospital. And, while I'm glad to know Suzanne didn't take her own life, I realize this was about me, not her. It's about me taking a risk and choosing love. Choosing you.' He took another breath. 'So, the question is, do you choose me?'

'Do I choose you?' Abby repeated, smiling, a hint of laughter, of incredulous hope and joy, in her voice. That night in Paris hadn't really been a choice, she saw now. It had been a fairy tale, the first awakening. Even in Cornwall, she'd simply reacted to the overwhelming attraction she felt for Luc; she'd been powerless in its pull. She still felt that now, but she also felt something deeper. Stronger. And she knew, absolutely knew, what choice to make.

'I choose you,' she said simply, and walked towards him. His arms came around her, pulling her gently yet firmly into an embrace that felt more like home than anything Abby had ever known.

A shrill, plaintive cry rent the air, and Luc smiled against her hair. 'And someone else is choosing too,' he murmured. 'To wake up, that is.'

Laughing, her fingers still threaded with Luc's, Abby went to care for their daughter.

EPILOGUE

Three months later

THE air was warm, yet with a hint of crispness, and the late September leaves were tinged with yellow as Luc drove the car up the drive. Chateau Mirabeau lay mellow and golden under the September sun, its window-panes gleaming and twinkling with sunlight, the last blooms of summer still filling the gardens, their scent heavy on the air.

Luc parked the car and reached for the car-seat in the back, where Emilie slept, one little fist lying curled next to her soft, round cheek. Abby climbed out of the passenger seat.

'Close your eyes,' Luc told her.

'For how long?'

'Till I say.' He reached out and took her by the hand, leading her across the gravel drive and up the front steps of the chateau. The door was open, and the air was fresh with the scent of polish and roses. Abby longed to open her eyes, to see all the changes Luc had wrought, but obediently she kept them closed.

'Where are you taking me?'

'You'll see.'

A little disoriented, Abby let him lead her through a maze of rooms, until finally he stopped. She could feel sunlight on her face, and somehow she just *knew*.

'Open them.'

She opened them slowly, blinking a little as she took in the refurbished music-salon. The magnificent Erard piano had been completely restored, and stood gold and gleaming. A few sofas and chairs were strategically placed around the room, perfect for an informal gathering or small concert. Abby stepped towards the piano. She hesitated, not having played properly in nearly eighteen months. Her fingers ached with the need to create music, to feel the smooth, ivory keys under their tips.

Luc waited, silently encouraging her, their daughter in his arms. And then Abby played. The music flowed like silk through the room, winding around them with its seductive melody. The *Apassionata*. But it no longer sounded sad to Abby.

It sounded passionate, even urgent, a joyful plea to live life. To enjoy it while you could. To be thankful. She closed her eyes, breathing the notes, living the music as if it were air, water, sustenance.

Luc didn't speak until the last note died away, and when Abby turned to him she felt tears on her cheeks. Happy tears. She wiped them away unashamedly, smiling at Luc.

'Thank you.'

'Thank *you*,' he replied, his voice low and heartfelt. Still smiling, Abby took him by the hand and led him out to the terrace, where they watched the sun send out its golden rays over the grassy meadows and the tangled vines of the Toussaint vineyard—the land that would one day belong to Emilie—all the way to the sleepy Rhône in the distance.

A bird cooed softly. Her heart full—wonderfully full—Abby knew all was right with the world.

LARGER-PRINT BOOKS!

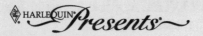